THE MARSHLAND MYSTERY

**Trixie
Belden**

Your TRIXIE BELDEN Library

Trixie Belden and the
MARSHLAND MYSTERY

BY KATHRYN KENNY

Cover by Jack Wacker

GOLDEN PRESS
Western Publishing Company, Inc.
Racine, Wisconsin

CONTENTS

THE MARSHLAND MYSTERY

Trixie Makes Plans · 1

BRIEF APRIL SHOWERS had been falling off and on since early morning, but now, as the junior-senior high school at Sleepyside-on-the-Hudson let out for the weekend, the skies were clear. Only a handful of white, fluffy clouds still decorated the horizon to the northwest, above the faraway Catskill Mountains.

Trixie Belden, her sandy, close-cropped curls dancing in a brisk little breeze, erupted from the wide doorway with the surge of boys and girls.

Trixie was bubbly, sturdy, thirteen-almost-fourteen, with round blue eyes which sparkled right now with excitement as she looked about eagerly for her very best friend, Honey Wheeler. She could hardly wait to tell Honey what she was planning for the next day.

But Honey was nowhere in sight. Usually they came out at the same time and met under the tallest of the maples beside the main walk. All Trixie could do was wait, fidgeting with impatience.

Honey was thirteen, too. Her home was out on Glen
Road, on a huge estate next to the modest farm that
the Beldens had lived on for generations. There were
woodlands, a lake, a stable of fine horses, and every
other luxury that her millionaire father could provide.
But she had been a lonely, unhappy girl until she had
met Trixie, less than a year before, when her parents
had bought Manor House.

The two girls had hit it off at once and had become
the closest of friends and partners in several adventures.
They both loved mysteries and had solved several
together.

The girls and their brothers were members of a secret
club they had started several months earlier. They called
themselves the Bob-Whites of the Glen, B.W.G.'s for
short. The club wasn't for fun alone; as Trixie's sixteen-
year-old brother, Brian, had said, "We're brothers and
sisters helping each other, as well as having good times."
And that's how it was working out. They had had some
exciting times together since they had started and had
worked hard to make a success of their club.

Trixie had just about made up her mind to go back
inside the building to see what was keeping Honey,
when she heard a teasing voice say, "Hi, small one! Why
the gleam in the cerulean orbs? Can it be there is mischief afoot in yon tangle-haired head?"

It was freckle-faced Mart, her "middle" brother. He
was grinning at her from the other side of the tree.

Trixie frowned. "My hair isn't tangled. It's naturally
curly, just the same as yours is when you don't have it
whacked off in that silly-looking crew cut!"

"Insults will get you nowhere, chickie. Come on, give out with the information. What's your latest brainstorm?" he teased.

But Trixie knew how to stop him. "Now, don't be a snoop, my dear little *twin brother!* Sister will tell you all about it later on."

If there was anything Mart hated, it was being called Trixie's twin. He was eleven months older, but they looked so much alike that people were always gushing over him and telling him that they could see he was a Belden—he looked so much like his twin sister, Trixie. Even having his hair clipped and standing tall didn't help; he was only an inch or so taller than Trixie.

His face reddened with irritation. "Forget it. I couldn't care less. It's probably some harebrained, dizzy idea like sending red flannel long johns to the Navahos."

He turned abruptly and swaggered off, swinging his load of books so violently at the end of their strap that books and papers flew in all directions. Mart had to scramble to gather them up before they were stepped on by the hurrying boys and girls.

Trixie held back an impulse to run and help him. She was really very fond of Mart, even if he could be a pest at times. The truth was that if she ever got herself into any sort of jam, Mart helped her out of it, though he grumbled and groused while he did it. Like last Christmas in Arizona, she thought, at the dude ranch. If Mart and Brian hadn't tutored her in both math and English during that holiday trip, she would have failed both subjects at school.

By the time she had decided to help pick up the books

and papers, Mart had them gathered together and was striding away toward the bus stop, and Honey and one of the other B.W.G.'s, pretty, dark-haired Diana Lynch, were coming hurriedly toward her.

"Hi! I thought you were going to spend the evening here!" Trixie greeted them. "Come on! We can catch the bus if we hurry. I've got something I want to tell you both."

"What's happened?" Honey asked eagerly. "Tell us right away!"

Honey was taller than either Trixie or Di, though she was a few weeks younger. She was slim and athletic and the best swimmer in the club. It was her wide hazel eyes and honey-colored hair that had earned her her nickname.

"Well, nothing yet," Trixie had to admit as the three hurriedly made their way through the milling crowd toward the bus stop. "But you can't tell what might happen!"

"It sounds exciting!" Di said. "Hurry and tell us!" Di was always ready to follow Trixie's ideas. She thought there was no one like Trixie. It was Trixie's love of mysteries that had helped Di's wealthy family to get rid of an impostor who had planned to rob them the previous Halloween.

"Well, this afternoon, in botany class—" Trixie began. Then she broke off. "Oh, gleeps! There goes the bus! We'll have to wait for the next one. And I wanted to tell Brian and ask him to go with us—"

"Where?" Honey asked. "If you don't tell us all about it, right this second, I'm going to stand here and scream as loud as I can! And I'll tell everybody you were torturing me!"

"And *I* will, too!" Di giggled.

But Trixie waited till they were seated on the bench at the bus stop before she continued. "It's a surprise for Miss Bennett," she began. "You remember what happened in botany class this afternoon, Di, when one of those goofy kids tripped over his own feet while he was carrying Miss Bennett's book of pressed herbs to the cabinet."

"They spilled all over, and everything got mixed up and broken," Di told Honey, who wasn't taking botany that term. "I felt so sorry for Miss Bennett. I thought for a minute she was going to cry when she saw the mess."

"But she didn't," Trixie said soberly. "She was awfully brave. She just said she knew Joel hadn't done it purposely, so there was no use getting upset. She let him sweep up all the dried leaves and flowers and throw them into her wastebasket."

"She can get new ones, can't she?" Honey frowned. "There must be plenty around."

"I suppose she could, if she didn't have rheumatism and have to walk with a cane. It must have taken her years to get her collection."

"But where do the B.W.G.'s come in?" Honey asked. "I'm sure none of us would know an herb from a weed."

"Brian does. It was in Miss Bennett's class that he first got the idea of becoming a doctor. He used to drag home armfuls of all sorts of weeds and swamp plants every weekend and spend most of Sunday cataloging them."

"Then if he still has his collection, why can't he give it

to Miss Bennett?" Honey asked eagerly.

Trixie shook her head and looked gloomy. "He doesn't have it anymore. Practically the same thing happened to it that happened to Miss Bennett's. Only it was Bobby who got into it and made hash out of it a few months ago."

Bobby was Trixie's six-year-old brother. There were few things he didn't get into, but there was no use in being angry with him, Trixie had found out. His naughtiness never lasted long, and he was always so sorry, that his big sister, who adored him, was quick to forgive him when the little boy's chubby arms went around her neck.

"I don't know anybody who has pressed plants and things," Di said regretfully. "Could we take some money from the club treasury and buy some for Miss Bennett?"

"I think Brian, as treasurer, would okay it," Trixie told her with a sigh, "only there's no place where you can buy them. You have to gather them yourself, in swamps and fields and among rocks."

"Oh!" Di looked disappointed. "Then what you're thinking about is our going someplace tomorrow and finding some specimens for her."

"That's it," Trixie told her with enthusiasm. "Brian could drive us in his jalopy and show us which ones are which. And Mart and Jim could help. And I guess Dan Mangan might get off, for just one day, from all the traps and things he takes care of for your gamekeeper, Honey."

Dan Mangan was the B.W.G.'s newest member, a city boy who had come to the country under a cloud of suspicion. But Dan, thanks to Trixie's detective work, had been cleared and had found a real home for himself.

"It should be fun," Honey said, but she had lost a lot of her first excitement. Gathering herbs didn't sound very thrilling. "I don't know about sloshing around in an oozy old swamp, though. Ugh!"

"We can stay on the paths. There are always paths in swamps," Trixie assured her. "Brian told me so."

"Well," Di sighed, "I suppose you can count me in."

"And the rest of us, I imagine." Honey smiled. "I'm sure *Jim* will think it's a great idea." Her eyes twinkled with mischief as she glanced at the identification bracelet on Trixie's wrist.

Trixie's cheeks got red as she flashed a reproachful look at her best friend, then pulled her sweater sleeve down over the inexpensive gift that Honey's adopted brother had given her after their adventurous Easter holiday on Trixie's uncle's farm in Iowa.

Honey and Di knew it wasn't really a sentimental gift, but they liked to make Trixie blush. Jim Frayne had been a runaway not too many months before, when Trixie and Honey had first met him. They had helped him escape from a brutal stepfather, and Jim had been deeply grateful. Now, adopted by the Wheelers, and himself the owner of an estate of half a million dollars, Jim was a senior at Sleepyside High and planned to go to college in the fall. After college, he intended to use his entire fortune to establish a home and school for homeless boys such as he himself had been.

All the B.W.G.'s were proud of Jim because, in spite of his wealth, he worked as hard as the Belden boys after school and on weekends. He and Trixie were co-presidents of the club, and it had been his idea that no

member could use money for the club that she or he
hadn't earned. So they all had jobs at home, for which
their parents paid them small regular salaries.

It wasn't easy to get schoolwork finished and attend
to their other jobs, too, but they managed somehow, and
each put something into the club treasury every week.

That was how the clubhouse had been fixed up out of
the old run-down gatehouse at the foot of the Wheeler
driveway. The gatehouse, almost hidden by wisteria and
honeysuckle vines, had been the scene of one of Trixie's
first mysteries. Now it was the neat, weathertight little
Bob-White clubhouse, thanks to many hours of hard
work by all the B.W.G.'s.

"Oh, well," Di sighed as the bus came along and
stopped, "I suppose we can wear old jeans and sneakers
in the swamp."

When they had crowded on with the rest of the boys
and girls, they were too late to find an empty seat.

"Oh, fine!" Trixie grumbled. "Now we stand for twenty
minutes, after a hard day's work!"

"Ow!" A football player had just stepped on Di's foot
as he pushed toward the rear.

Honey giggled. "Maybe this kind of thing builds character!" she suggested as the bus picked up speed and
hurtled around a corner, jiggling everyone.

It wasn't until they had limped out at the Wheeler
bus stop that they took a free breath.

"Whew! Now I know how a sardine feels!" Di groaned.

"Do you suppose that's what they mean by 'together-
ness'?" Honey laughed as she straightened the skirt of
her pretty spring dress.

They were still laughing when they noticed Mart sprawled out nonchalantly on the bench.

"Where have you squaws been?" he demanded. "Don't you know you all have chores waiting? Two demerits each for stopping for ice-cream bars!"

"We didn't," Trixie answered pertly. "We were planning an exciting trip for tomorrow, and since you're the only B.W.G. around, I suppose we'll have to tell you about it before we tell the intelligent ones."

"Trip?" Mart stirred lazily and got up. "So?"

Di smiled warmly at him. "To gather herbs in a swamp. And you and Jim and Brian are invited, too. Tell him, Trixie."

But before Trixie could start, Mart put up a warning hand. "Stop right there, dreamer. This is *the end*. Tomorrow we males are booked to labor from dawn till sundown. Hast forgotten that this is the time of planting? In other words, didn't you hear Dad tell Brian we'd put in Mr. Maypenny's corn tomorrow?"

"Yipes! I forgot all about it!" Trixie frowned. "And we were counting on getting Brian to take us in his car!"

"Something tells me, squaw, you won't get far from the family tepee tomorrow, unless you bike your way." Mart chortled. "Dan will be working all day and so will Jim."

"I guess we could bike, if the swamp isn't too far," Honey said, a frown on her pretty forehead. "If it's a long way, I suppose we'd better give up the idea. Don't you think so, Trix?"

"No!" Trixie set her jaw stubbornly. "And if nobody else wants to go, I'm going alone."

Mart took a quick look at his sister's expression and knew that she meant it. He had seen that look before. "Just where is the swamp you're heading for?" he asked, a little more seriously.

"Miss Bennett said most of her plant specimens came from Sedley Swamp. That's where we're going."

"Sedley Swamp?" Mart exclaimed. Then he shouted with laughter. "My dear lame-brained sister, there ain't no sich animal. Sedley Swamp is no more. It is now part of our new concrete superhighway!"

Strange Visitors · 2

OH, NO! YOU'RE JUST trying to be funny, Mart Belden!" Trixie accused her brother.

"Don't tease, Mart," Honey seconded her. "Really, we're very serious about gathering some plants out there tomorrow for Miss Bennett."

"If you are," Mart said, still amused, "you'll have to dig down under a few feet of concrete before you find Sedley Swamp. It has faded into history."

"Well," Trixie sighed, "I suppose that's that. And I had such big plans for walking into botany room Monday with my arms full of milkweed and bee balm!"

"Now you'll have to study, instead of trying to get good marks by buttering up Miss Bennett," Mart continued teasingly.

Trixie flashed him an annoyed look. "We weren't buttering her up at all." Then she explained about the destruction of the teacher's prize specimens.

Honey added the last word. "So, you see, Trixie was

being very unselfish, Mart. And it was her own idea, not
Di's or mine."

"Very noble, I'm sure," Mart agreed, "but why do you
busy little bees have to gather the plants from one
special swamp? Won't any other one do?"

"Of course. Only I never heard of another swamp
within biking distance," Trixie said promptly.

"There *is* one, but you probably didn't think of it as a
swamp. It's called Martin's Marsh, but that would convey
nothing to you, dear sister, because you, with your complete lack of familiarity with your native tongue, could
hardly be expected to realize that *marsh* is simply a
synonym for *swamp*."

Trixie sniffed. "I happen to know that marshes and
swamps are practically the same, but I never heard of
any Martin's Marsh—and I bet you made up the name."

"I wish you'd mean it even half the times you say
'I bet,'" Mart chuckled. "I'd be rich with all the money
I'd win from you. It just happens that it's about a half
mile east of Sleepyside, beyond the old Martin Manor
House ruins. Brian gathered most of his specimens there
when he was taking botany."

"Oh, good!" Honey said quickly. "You can ask him
how to get there, Trixie!"

"And find out which plants should be blooming there
now, this early in the season," Di added. "I've heard
that some herbs should be gathered in spring and others
when they're in bloom in July or August. And some you
shouldn't pick till they go to seed—and—" She was getting
interested in the project now.

"Brian knows all the answers," Mart interrupted. He

glanced at his wristwatch. "But if you intend to ask him anything, Trix, you'd better scoot off home, quick like a rabbit, and do it before he gets too deep in his Latin. He has to study all evening to make up for taking the day off tomorrow to help with the planting."

"I'll be on my way right now," Trixie assured him. And to the girls she said hastily, "I'll phone you both the very minute I've talked to Brian. Then you can talk to your folks and arrange for the trip. Don't forget to remind them it's really part of our schoolwork."

"Mom is having some people at the house for a few days," Honey said, a little frown creasing her forehead, "but I'm sure they aren't any of our relatives or anybody she'd want me to stay home and entertain. I can't remember who they are. Some foreign name, I think. Something to do with the Arts Club that Mom's president of."

"I don't think I'm doing anything special this weekend," Di said, "so I won't have much trouble getting away."

"Wonderful! Don't go far from the phone, and I'll call just as soon as I can."

Trixie shifted her load of books to her other hip and started off along Glen Road toward the small white Belden farmhouse. Mart caught up with her in a couple of strides, and they hurried along in silence for a few minutes.

"Pretty decent of you to want to cheer up the old girl with some new specimens," Mart said finally.

Trixie was so startled by the unexpected compliment that she came to a complete stop and stood staring at her almost-twin in amazement. "Well!" she finally managed to get out. "Thanks!" And she meant it.

Mart frowned at her. "Come on! Moms is probably having fits, because you promised to get home early and take Bobby off her hands so she could go shopping."

"Ouch! I forgot!" Hurrying after Mart, she fell into stride with him, and they went along together again in comfortable silence.

A small warm wind sent the faint perfume of crab apple blossoms along Glen Road from the Belden orchard.

"Mmm! Smell that!" Trixie broke the silence.

Mart sniffed the air. "Hmf! It's just gasoline fumes."

"You know I didn't mean that, Mart Belden," Trixie snapped irritably and stalked on.

Mart chuckled. "How would anyone know what goes on in that infinitesimal think tank of yours?"

Trixie had a retort on the tip of her tongue, but they had reached the foot of their home driveway, and what she saw up in front of the small white farmhouse stopped her. It stopped Mart, too.

For a moment they both stood staring at the three expensive cars that were parked there.

"Oh, Mart! Something must have happened!" Trixie's quick mind went to work. "Maybe Bobby ran out in front of one of the cars or Brian bumped his jalopy into one of them. Let's hurry!"

Mart took hold of her arm quickly. "Whoa, there! Don't push the panic button! It's probably the Landmarks Society examining our pegged floors again. You know, we're quite historical—or should I say *hysterical*, at the moment?"

Trixie pulled, but Mart held on, and a minute later she stopped struggling. "All right. I'm calm. I'm sure it's all right, or those three drivers wouldn't be just standing around talking behind that second car."

They were both walking at a dignified pace as they came past the three limousines lined up near the house.

"I don't hear any chattering going on inside, do you?" Mart asked. "Wonder what the ladies are looking at this time. Could be the old butter churn out on the back porch."

"Let's go look." Trixie hurried on.

But there was no one there, either. Trixie, poking her head in at the kitchen door, saw signs of interrupted dinner preparations but no Moms.

Mart was close on her heels. "Mysteriouser and mysteriouser," he hissed, helping himself to a red-cheeked apple from the dish that always stood in the center of the table. But he had no time to bite into it. Voices from a distance were being wafted to their ears from somewhere out in the crab apple orchard behind the house.

Mart dashed back to the door and started out. "Hey! Looks like a convention. Something's going on out under the trees. I can see Moms and Bobby watching."

Trixie hardly waited for him to finish speaking before she was on her way out. Mart and the apple followed.

The crab apple trees were a mass of blooms against the clear blue of the afternoon sky. Trixie had been admiring them every morning for the past week, after they had all burst into bloom at practically the same time, so her attention was all on the strangers in the orchard.

A man had set up a camera on a tripod and was
apparently getting ready to photograph a small girl
dressed in a vivid costume and holding a violin in her
hand. She was very slight and frail-looking, with long
golden curls. Trixie decided that she must be about
seven years old, eight, at the most. She was standing
quietly while three women fussed over her curls,
powdered her nose, and adjusted her costume. The only
time she moved was when a stray blossom, loosened by
the wind, floated down and landed on her cheek. Then
she brushed it away impatiently and stood woodenly
again, looking bored.

It was Mart who spotted the lettering on the photographer's satchel: SLEEPYSIDE SUN.

"Publicity stuff," Mart told a puzzled Trixie. "I don't
know who Goldilocks is, but it looks as if the *Sleepyside
Sun* thinks she's worth a picture. I hope Moms is charging
rental on the crab apple trees!"

"Why, she wouldn't—" Trixie stopped abruptly as she
saw that Mart was just fooling. But a moment later,
after studying the delicate-looking child a little more,
she said thoughtfully, "I know I've seen her before
somewhere."

"Maybe you've been visiting a gypsy camp, looking
for a clue to one of your mysteries. All those beads and
the bright-colored clothes look like a gypsy outfit."

"But she's a blonde, and those long yellow curls don't
belong on a gypsy," Trixie whispered back.

They moved closer to Moms and Bobby and stood
watching in silence as a young man stepped up to one
of the three women who had been fussing over the child.

"We'd like another shot of her playing the violin, if you don't mind, Miss Crandall. The light is just right now," the young man said eagerly, "for a backlight effect."

"Very well, Mr. Trent." The tall, severe-faced woman snapped her words. "But only *one* more. And hurry with it. My niece is getting tired."

"Thanks, Miss Crandall." He and the photographer hurried to the little girl. "How about a pretty smile this time, Gaye?" he coaxed.

The little girl gave him a cold, unfriendly look. "I'm tired, and I don't feel like smiling," she told him. "Just finish, and then go away."

"That's telling him!" Mart told Trixie with a grin. He hadn't intended to speak loudly enough to be heard by anyone but Trixie, but it happened to be one of those strangely quiet moments when no one else was speaking. As a consequence, several of the others turned startled faces toward him, and Mart's freckled face flushed crimson.

The young reporter scowled at Mart, but the photographer laughed. "Okay, sis. This is the last," he told the little girl good-naturedly and prepared to take the picture.

"Who are they, Moms?" Trixie whispered.

"Guests of the Wheelers. That young man from the *Sun* is preparing an article about the little girl. She's a famous violinist, I understand."

Trixie was impressed but puzzled. "But she's awfully little to be famous! She can't be much older than Bobby." She frowned. "Why did they come here to take pictures?"

Mrs. Belden smiled. "Our crab apple trees are the prettiest background they could find, and Mrs. Wheeler suggested it. They're staying for tea, so you'd better hurry in and get the kettle on. We'll use the best china."

The picture was taken now, and the child was standing alone. Trixie had a sudden impulse to go to her and ask her to come along into the house and help get tea ready.

But before she could reach her, Trixie's good-natured Irish setter, Reddy, came loping in, tongue lolling, tail wagging, from some business of his own in the woods. He saw the small blond girl and ventured over to investigate her. The little girl gave a terrified scream and dropped the violin.

In answer to her scream, a small white poodle hurtled suddenly out of the open door of one of the big cars in the driveway. Barking shrilly, he dashed to the rescue, with all the courage of a lion.

Reddy stopped to look at the tiny white ball of fur rushing noisily at him, and he got down on his haunches to challenge it to a romp. The poodle skidded to a stop at a safe distance but continued its shrill yelps of defiance.

Sunlight flashed on the small dog's brilliant collar. Mart laughed. "Look out, Reddy," he called, "or that city dude will chew you to pieces!"

"No! No! Don't you hurt Mr. Poo!" the little girl shrieked and started to run toward the two animals.

"Gaye! Come back here!" Miss Crandall called, hurrying after the child. "You'll be hurt! Remember your hands!"

But Gaye kept on going. Then she tripped and fell,

and the shrieks changed to screams of anger and pain.

Trixie dashed toward Reddy to pull him away from the yapping poodle, but Reddy dodged and escaped her. Encouraged, the poodle chased after Reddy, and Reddy galumphed around happily, with the poodle yapping at his heels. It was all a lovely romp for good-natured Reddy, and the tiny poodle seemed to be beginning to enjoy the chase.

Mart laughed. "Wish I had my camera," he said as Trixie stood watching the two dogs disappear into the orchard. Trixie tried to think of something withering to say about his sense of humor but gave it up after a futile moment.

"Go get that little dog and tie Reddy up," her mother called hastily as she went by, with Bobby in tow, to help the ladies soothe the screaming Gaye.

"Mart, would you?" Trixie coaxed.

Mart shook his head firmly. "Reddy's your dog. Scoot, before Reddy gets tired of having his ears blasted by that insect's shrieks and gets himself a poodle leg for supper!"

"Reddy wouldn't do such a thing!" Trixie snapped. But as she hurried after the two dogs, she wasn't nearly as certain as she had pretended to be that the big red setter wouldn't forget his manners and take a nip at the pesky yipper.

She lost sight of the pair almost as soon as she entered the orchard, but she could still hear the poodle barking in the distance. She cupped her hands around her mouth and called, "Reddy! Come back here!" Usually Reddy barked when he heard his name called, but this time there wasn't a sound from him. And now the poodle had stopped its shrill barking, too.

She could see where they had romped across last year's damp leaves. There was a trail she could easily follow, and she lost no time taking it, calling as she went.

Then, not far ahead, she heard Reddy's bark. It was sharp. He barked the way he did when he had treed a porcupine or located a woodchuck hole. It was his hunting bark.

Trixie broke into a run. She hoped Reddy hadn't decided that the white poodle was something to be hunted!

But when she came in sight of the big red dog, she saw how wrong she had been. He was standing between the tiny white poodle and something among the leaves at the foot of a tall tree.

With a menacing growl and bared teeth, Reddy was moving slowly toward a coiled and hissing snake that was almost the color of the faded leaves.

It was a deadly copperhead.

Small Genius · 3

TRIXIE KNEW THAT one blow from the deadly copperhead's fangs on Reddy's long nose would be fatal. Her dog was not trained to hunt snakes. He would approach to attack it head on, as he would a badger or a wildcat. The snake would strike before Reddy could seize it. "Reddy! Here, Reddy!" she yelled desperately.

The big setter stopped his slow progress to glance back uncertainly at her. She called again, "Come!" as sharply as she could.

Training took over then, and Reddy turned back toward his mistress. Among the dead leaves at the foot of the tree, the snake uncoiled and slithered away.

"Good boy!" Trixie's voice shook in spite of her efforts to keep it steady. Reddy's long, plumed tail swung happily.

But now the tiny poodle was starting toward the tree, his small black nose quivering with curiosity.

"Mr. Poo!" Trixie let go of Reddy and made a dive for

the poodle. She caught him up and held him safe, in
spite of his wriggles. "We're leaving right now, you two
trouble hunters!" she told Reddy and the poodle. "Come
on, Reddy. Big bone waiting!" She led them back through
the orchard.

As soon as she saw her father tonight, she thought,
she'd be sure to tell him about the copperhead, and he
and Brian could come out armed with heavy sticks and
flush it out of the leaves. The reptiles were sluggish and
moved slowly, so it would not be far from here. There
were several big boulders at the far end of the orchard,
and very likely it had a den there. Every spring a few
of the snakes were seen around the farm, and every
spring her father and the boys made a project of ridding
the place of them. Since Bobby's experience with a copperhead the summer before, she knew that they'd act
quickly about this intruder.

Trixie came hurriedly back to the edge of the orchard,
with the poodle nestling contentedly in her arms and
Reddy close at her heels.

The reporter and the cameraman were just leaving
in one of the cars. Miss Crandall called sharply after the
young reporter, "I must approve all photographs before
they are printed, Mr. Trent. Don't forget."

"Sure thing, Miss Crandall. We'll have them ready
for your okay tomorrow." He spoke to the driver, and
they drove away.

Miss Crandall had her niece firmly by the hand, and
the governess was putting the violin away in its case.

The little girl was rubbing her eyes and sobbing
quietly as Trixie came up behind them. She looked

forlorn and unhappy, and Trixie had an impulse to cheer her.

"Hey, there! Here's your puppy, Gaye!" she called. "Here's Mr. Poo, all safe and happy."

Gaye looked quickly, dashing away her tears. Then she snatched her hand from her aunt's and ran toward Trixie, exclaiming, "Give him to me! He's mine!"

Trixie snuggled her nose in the poodle's topknot by way of farewell and then held him out to Gaye. "He's a darling."

Gaye's eyes flashed with jealousy and anger as she snatched the little animal from Trixie. "Let go of him! He doesn't want to be with you! I'm the only one he loves!" She was hugging the puppy so hard that he let out a small yip of distress and struggled to get away. "He's mine!" She began to cry loudly and hugged him even tighter, in spite of his wriggling.

Mrs. Belden hurried to Gaye and put her arms around the child. "It's all right, dear. Trixie wasn't trying to keep him. She brought him back to you."

"Then send her away!" Gaye demanded, glaring at Trixie defiantly. Mrs. Belden hastily motioned to Trixie to go.

Trixie was annoyed. The little monster! And after she had practically saved the puppy's life! She turned away with a frown and almost bumped into Mart and Brian, who were watching the scene with amused grins.

"Dognapping, hey? What next?" Mart teased. "And from such a sweet little girl!" He wrinkled his nose at Trixie and grinned.

"If you want to know," Trixie told him with great

dignity, "I probably saved his yippy little life."

"From being squeezed to death?" Brian smiled.

"No. From a copperhead," Trixie told him. And both boys sobered at once as she explained.

"Good girl," Brian said grimly. "We'll take care of Mr. Copperhead tomorrow. Meanwhile, keep Bobby out of the orchard."

Behind them, Miss Crandall's voice came sharply. "Stop the sniveling at once, or I'll send that dog to a boarding kennel tomorrow. I won't have you getting all worked up when you have a concert to give!"

Gaye wailed loudly. "Please, Aunt Della! I won't cry. Don't take him away! Please!"

"Poor kid!" Brian muttered under his breath.

The three of them watched Miss Crandall take the puppy out of Gaye's clinging arms and hand him to the governess. "Put him in the car till we're ready to go."

Gaye screamed after the governess, "Don't let anybody touch him!"

"Recognize the little princess yet?" Mart grinned.

Trixie nodded. "I just this minute remembered. I saw her picture on a poster in front of the Music Hall last week when Mrs. Wheeler took Honey and me to hear the string quartet. She's Gaye Hunya, and she's going to play the violin there next Saturday."

"Not just 'play the violin,' Trix," Brian told her. "Our temperamental little friend is to appear as guest soloist with the symphony. And she gave a recital at Carnegie Hall when she was only five years old. Her father was a famous European violinist."

"Well, bully for her!" Mart said dryly. "Too bad she

isn't a singer instead of a fiddler. She can scream loud enough when she wants to!"

"What a life she must lead," Brian said thoughtfully.

Trixie stared at him, puzzled. He sounded as if he were actually sorry for the little prodigy. "I should think it would be simply super to be famous and have people buying thousands of tickets to hear you."

"It's also hard work," Mart reminded her, "which would not be so popular with *you!*"

"I work just as hard as you do, Mart Belden," Trixie retorted. "All you do is a few chores and exercise the Wheeler horses. And I do that and a lot more—taking care of Bobby when Moms is busy and doing the dishes and everything else!"

"For which you collect handsomely, to the extent of five legal simoleons per week. Pretty neat!" Mart gibed.

"Most of which she puts into the B.W.G. treasury," Brian reminded him, with a mischievous sparkle in his dark eyes. "Not like some people I could mention."

Mart's color flared. "Just because I held out two measly dollars last week—" he exploded. Then he saw that they were both laughing, and he grinned with them. "I had to buy Dad a new tie because I spilled catsup on the one I borrowed from him, and it wasn't washable."

"Washable catsup. Now, that's something I haven't seen yet. Have you, Trixie?" Brian teased.

Trixie giggled. She was enjoying herself because Brian was giving Mart the same kind of teasing that her almost-twin usually gave her.

"Trixie, dear! Will you come here?" It was Moms. She still had her arm around Gaye's shoulders and was

starting toward the house with the little girl and her
aunt and the other two women.

"Okay, Moms," Trixie called. Then hastily she asked
Brian, "Did Mart tell you about what we're going to do
tomorrow?"

Brian nodded. "I'll draw you kids a map, so you won't
end up in the Hudson River instead of Martin's Marsh.
Wish we could drive you there, but we're tied up. Mart
told you about that, I guess."

Trixie nodded. "Would he ever miss telling me bad
news?" she asked, with a grimace at Mart. "Thanks,
Brian."

Then she hurried to join Moms.

"Dear, would you take Gaye to your room and let
her freshen up?"

Trixie looked at Gaye and made herself smile. Gaye
looked bored. "Come along, Gaye." The little girl, with
a tiny shrug of her shoulders, followed Trixie to the
house.

Trixie wasn't aware for a minute or two that Bobby
was tagging along, until he started up the stairs close
on their heels.

"Where do you think you're going?" She smiled at
Bobby while Gaye went on ahead. "Run back to Moms,
and we'll be with you soon."

"But I wanna give her a plesent," he insisted, "because she's so pretty." He held a rather grimy small box
tightly in one hand.

"What is it?" Trixie asked suspiciously, knowing
Bobby. The "plesent" might be anything from a collection of rocks to a garter snake. She reached for the box.

"No, it's for her." Bobby held it away. "You mustn't take it."

"Let me look at it, Bobby!" Trixie frowned.

But Bobby, shaking his head vigorously, darted past her and up the stairs to the landing, where Gaye was waiting.

"Here!" He thrust the box at Gaye. "It's Oscar!"

Trixie gasped. She knew who Oscar was. "Oh, no!" she exclaimed and started up the stairs again to stop Gaye from opening the box. "Don't take it!"

But Gaye held the box behind her and looked haughtily at Trixie. "He gave it to *me!* Didn't you, boy?"

Bobby nodded vigorously while he stared admiringly at Gaye and shyly thrust a thumb into his mouth.

Gaye started to open the box, and Trixie got ready for a scream. She was surprised when Gaye, after cautiously peeking into the partially open box, closed it again and smiled at Bobby. "A darling little chameleon! And you're giving it to me!"

"Because you're pretty," Bobby said, continuing to admire her.

"Well, thank you," Gaye said in a very sweet voice that was a startling change from the one she had used in speaking to Trixie. "Now, be a good boy, and I'll give you one of my latest photos."

Bobby took the thumb out of his mouth long enough to say, "Awright! I'll wait for you!" Then he scooted downstairs, grinning happily.

Trixie swallowed hard. After all the hours she put in taking care of him and reading him to sleep each night, a head of blond curls had won his heart! She went up

the stairs to Gaye. "Come on, I'll take you to my room,"
she told Gaye abruptly as she passed her.

"First, get rid of this horrible thing!" Gaye thrust the
box and its contents at Trixie. "Aren't small children a
nuisance? They bore me."

Trixie took the box without answering. She felt a
temptation to remind Gaye that, prodigy or not, she was
only a small child herself—and pretty much of a monster,
too!

Then, as they entered Trixie's neat little bedroom and
Trixie saw Gaye look about her with scornful eyes, she
had a horrible thought. Gaye was staying at Honey's
house. That could mean that Honey would be stuck
with her tomorrow and they couldn't take their trip to
Martin's Marsh. Neither she nor Di would have as much
fun without Honey along, so the expedition would have
to be postponed. And next Saturday would probably
be the same.

The world seemed suddenly very dark indeed to
Trixie—and all on account of a golden-haired virtuosa
of the violin.

The Expedition • 4

AFTER THE VISITORS had left for the Wheelers', Trixie began to feel better. A quick call to Honey revealed that her mother saw no reason why Honey should stay home the next day to entertain the little girl. Gaye would have to practice most of the day, as she had to do before every concert, so Honey would be free.

Di wasn't so lucky. Her mother had planned a day of shopping in White Plains with her, and Di had to go. She wailed about it over the phone to Trixie.

Trixie hesitated. They'd have more fun if they all went next Saturday. But suppose Honey were busy then, or she was. She decided she'd have to take that chance. "Okay, Di. We'll put it off—"

Di interrupted, "Hold on a minute." There was a murmur of voices from Di's end of the line as Trixie held on. Then Di came back on the phone. "There's no use in your upsetting your plans, Trix. Mom says next week we're taking both pairs of twins to Grandma's for a visit. So you and Honey go ahead and have fun."

Trixie felt guilty about being relieved that she and Honey wouldn't have to put off the little expedition. "Tell you what, Di," she said hastily. "Whatever we bring back, half is for you to take to class. I'm sure we'll get loads of specimens. Brian's going to make us a list of what to look for, and he'll even draw some pictures of them so we won't miss them!"

"Oh, thanks, Trix! You're the best," Di assured her.

"Well, kiss the twins for me," Trixie told her as she hung up. The two pairs of twins were still small, and though the Lynches were very wealthy and had two nurses to care for them, Di received an extra allowance for taking the nurses' places on their days off. It was fun, and it gave her something to contribute to the Bob-Whites' treasury every week.

Trixie awoke early next morning and at once made a dash for the window to see if the weather was good. The ground was damp, but the sky was clear, except for a few fleecy clouds that moved rapidly away to the west.

"Thank goodness it rained during the night and got it over with!" she thought, dressing hurriedly in her jeans and a stout pair of brogans. She would have preferred sneakers, because they didn't tire her when she hiked, but Moms had made her promise to wear waterproofs on this expedition because it would undoubtedly be damp underfoot in the marsh.

The house seemed very quiet, and Trixie decided that she must be the first one up. She tiptoed around getting dressed, making as little noise as possible because she didn't want to wake Bobby. He would be sure to want to go with them, and it just wasn't possible.

She tiptoed out of her room and down the hall. She had some chores to do, like feeding the chickens and gathering the newly laid eggs. That wouldn't take long. Usually she had dishes to wash and beds to make as part of her duties, but Moms had offered to do them today to help her out.

She pushed open the kitchen door and was surprised to see her mother and father having breakfast. Her dad wore a warm shirt and heavy overalls.

"Well, dear, you're up early. There's some hot cereal on the stove, and I've fixed a good lunch for you and Honey." Her mother pointed to a packed basket that was waiting on the sink.

"Thanks heaps, Moms," Trixie said gratefully. "I didn't think anybody'd be awake yet."

"We've all been up quite a while, except for Bobby. I'm letting him sleep," her mother explained.

"You mean Brian and Mart are gone already?" Trixie asked, dismayed. "Brian promised—"

Her mother smiled and nodded toward a sheet of paper propped up against the lunch basket. "He kept his promise. There's your map, carefully marked. And he's added a list of swamp plants you'll find at this time of year. Also a few landmarks, so you can't possibly miss your way."

Trixie dashed over and got the paper. The map was drawn with Brian's usual neatness. Not only was their route marked, but also how far they had to go along each section of it before coming to a turn. "This is super!" Trixie announced happily. "We'll whiz right out there without a bit of trouble. Brian's a doll!"

"I'm sure he'd enjoy that description!" Mr. Belden laughed. He was dark, like Brian, and usually quite serious. Trixie supposed it was because he had such a responsible job at the Sleepyside Bank, and maybe people didn't think bankers should have a sense of humor. At least, that's what Mart had told her.

"Don't work too hard, dear," Mrs. Belden reminded her husband as he kissed her and started for the door. "Remember, you have your own planting to do after you help Mr. Maypenny and the boys!"

"You know we'll spend half the time resting!" he chuckled. Then, as Trixie bustled about getting ready for her trip, he paused in the doorway. "Remember, we want you back here before dark. No excuses."

"Of course, Dad!" Trixie assured him. "Have you ever been to the marsh yourself?"

"Several times," he told her, "but not for quite a while. It's quite a historic spot."

"Really?" Trixie was surprised. "Did an Indian massacre happen there? Was it a battlefield during the Revolution?"

"Neither. The legend is that Captain Kidd, the notorious pirate, was a friend and business partner of old Ezarach Martin, who owned all the land for miles around the swamp. So it was natural to suspect that Kidd buried a lot of his treasure in the swamp."

Trixie gasped. "Maybe we'll find some of his loot!"

Her father smiled. "Hardly possible. He was executed

two hundred and fifty years ago, and I'm quite sure that since then at least two hundred and fifty treasure hunters have dug in that swamp, without finding anything but mud and frogs."

"Didn't anyone find the least bit of pirate gold?" Trixie hated to give up.

"Not a trace of it. And worse than that—" he paused and looked mysterious—"I've heard that some of the diggers saw Captain Kidd's ghost flitting about through the marsh at midnight now and again. So you be sure to start for home before sundown."

"Br-r-r! We certainly will!" Trixie laughed. She knew that there was no such thing as a ghost and that her father was just joking.

After her father had left for the Maypenny farm in the station wagon, Trixie dashed out and gathered the eggs and fed the hens.

When she brought in the eggs, her mother told her quickly, "I hear Bobby running around upstairs, dear. You'd better be on your way before he discovers you intend to desert him. You know what a fuss he'll make."

"I'm on my way!" She snatched up the lunch basket, gave her mother a good-bye kiss, and was turning to go, when she remembered something. "Oh, I almost forgot! Did Brian tell you about the copperhead?"

"Yes, dear. They went out and took care of him and two others. I don't think we'll be bothered the rest of the season."

"That's fine." Trixie was relieved. "Well, so long, Moms. We'll be back early." This time she got as far as the door before she stopped. "I sort of hate to run off and leave you with all the work and Bobby, too," she said weakly.

Moms smiled. "Don't worry about it, dear. Bobby and I will be going over to Wheelers' a little later. Gaye has promised Bobby a picture of herself, and I gave him my word at bedtime that I'd take him there this morning."

Trixie frowned. "Moms—" she started to say and then hesitated.

Mrs. Belden could see that something was troubling Trixie. "What is it?"

Trixie swallowed hard. "Moms, don't you think Gaye is *awfully* spoiled? She was positively rude about my room. And she said our Bob-White jackets were corny."

"That's only *her* opinion. Why should it worry you, dear? She's just a little girl, hardly older than Bobby. And don't forget that she leads a very different life from the one you girls and boys live here. I doubt that the poor child has a real home and friends her own age."

"Just the same," Trixie said stubbornly, "she doesn't have to be so snippy. And she says one thing and means something else—like pretending, sweet as pie, that she liked Bobby's chameleon that he gave her and then telling me it was horrible."

Mrs. Belden smiled. "That's what people call a 'polite fib,' dear. It isn't quite honest, but I imagine Gaye didn't want to hurt Bobby's feelings by telling him how she really felt."

"Well"—Trixie frowned—"anyhow, she doesn't have to be so la-di-da and turn up her nose at other people's things."

"I'm sure she'll get over that after she's become used to you and Honey. The three of you will be friends in no time at all." Her mother saw that Trixie was still looking stubborn and told her gently, "I'm expecting you to be kind to the poor little girl. Promise?"

Trixie ran back to her mother and gave her a hug. "Oh, Moms! You can always find excuses for people, and then I realize I'm a monster. I'll try to like Gaye. I promise."

"Good girl! Now run along, or Honey will think you've changed your mind about exploring the marsh."

The clubhouse door was open as Trixie pedaled along Glen Road to the foot of the Wheeler driveway. Trixie felt the thrill she always experienced when she looked at the neat little cottage with its well-trained wisteria and honeysuckle vines. And, as usual, she reflected that the Bob-Whites had done a good job of fixing up the old gatehouse. It had taken plenty of work, but it had been worth it.

Trixie dismounted and went in. Jim was kneeling beside Honey's bike, putting a tire on the rear rim. Honey, watching, was handing him the tools.

"What happened?" Trixie asked quickly.

"I picked up an old nail somewhere," Honey explained, "but Jim's putting one of his own tires on."

"Well, hurry it up." Trixie waved her hand airily. "We ladies have a date with Captain Kidd's ghost at Martin's Marsh!"

Jim grinned broadly and shook his tire iron at Trixie. "You get sassy with me, small fry, and I'll tell Regan I've decided not to exercise your horse for you this morning. You know what'll happen then!"

Trixie clapped her hands to her head and groaned.

"*Do* I? He'll insist on my taking Susie for an extra-long run, and we'll never get started for the marsh!"

"Stop teasing Trixie, Jim." Honey laughed. "Don't let him scare you, Trix. We've had both Starlight and Susie out for a canter already."

"I went along," a sharp little voice said. "I rode Lady."

Gaye, looking very neat in an expensive riding outfit, leaned in the doorway, watching them coolly.

Trixie was surprised, but Honey said promptly, "That's right. Gaye's a splendid rider."

"I learned at the best school in Paris," the little girl said grandly, "and *they* had really *fine* horses, not like these slowpokes here."

Trixie's face flushed with indignation, and she turned to Jim and Honey, expecting them to defend their horses. But Honey was smiling indulgently at Gaye, and Jim was chuckling as he finished with the bike.

"I imagine they did, at that," Jim agreed blithely. He handed the bike over to Honey. "There you are, Honey. Have a grand time, and don't fall into the swamp." He turned to Trixie. "Did Brian give you the map?"

"He left it for me." Trixie fished the folded map out of her pocket and handed it to him. "It's a whiz!"

Jim glanced at it. "I'll say! Very neat, indeed. He practically leads you by the hand and tells you what to look for when you arrive. Good old Brian!"

Gaye stepped over and thrust her head between Jim and Honey to stare at the map. "Why are you going there?"

"To pick some flowers," Trixie answered shortly. "Very

special ones that you wouldn't know about."

Gaye looked up at her impudently. "I think I'll ask Aunt Della to let me go with you!" she announced.

"But it's—" Trixie started, with a frown. She stopped as she caught Honey's eye and Honey shook her head warningly. Trixie finished lamely, "It's too far for you."

"I guess I can do it if you can." Gaye scowled, and she turned to Honey. "May I ask her, Honey?"

"Go ahead, but hurry. We have to get started," Honey told her hastily.

Gaye darted out of the clubhouse, and they could hear her running up the cement driveway.

"Oh, Honey!" Trixie groaned. "You know she'll be a worse nuisance than Bobby! Besides, she doesn't have a bike, and we'll have to take turns letting her use ours!"

"Don't worry," Honey said calmly. "I heard Miss Crandall tell the governess that Gaye must start practicing the sonata by ten o'clock sharp. There's no chance of her tagging along with us."

"Then why do we wait? It's getting late," Trixie reminded her friend, "and I promised Daddy we'd be home before dark, without fail."

Honey looked troubled. "But I practically told her we'd wait until she had asked her aunt." She looked appealingly at her adopted brother. Whenever Honey had to make an important decision, she liked to get Jim's advice. "What do you think we'd better do?" she asked him.

"Simple. Just go on, you kids. It's so close to ten o'clock now that I doubt if her aunt even lets her come back here to tell you she can't go with you. I'll be busy here for a few minutes, and if she does show up, I'll tell her the truth. You knew she had to practice, so you didn't wait, but you were sorry she couldn't go. If she gets angry, she'll get over it." He waved them on.

"That makes sense," Trixie agreed with a grin. "Come on, Honey." And she was mounted on her bike and on her way in a minute.

As they cycled, side by side, along Glen Road toward the first turnoff that Brian had marked on the map, Trixie was more silent than usual. She was wrestling with her conscience. She had promised Moms that she would be kind to little Gaye, and she had meant to be. But she had an uneasy feeling that running off the way they had would show the child that they hadn't wanted her along, or they'd have waited for her and told her they were disappointed she couldn't come.

"There's the old Telegraph Road up ahead, I think," Honey called, "where that car just crossed. Does the map say we go east or west on it?"

"I'll check and see." Trixie reached into her pocket and kept on pedaling. "I don't remember."

"Neither do I," Honey admitted with a giggle that broke off suddenly when she saw the look on Trixie's face as Trixie braked her bike suddenly and felt frantically first in one pocket of her jacket and then the other. "What's the matter?"

"The map," Trixie told her glumly, giving up the search. "Jim didn't give it back to me. Now what are we going to do?"

A Face at the Window • 5

GLEEPS! I HATE to turn back now, but I suppose we'll have to." Trixie leaned dejectedly against her bicycle. "Without that map, we're sunk."

"Maybe there's some kind of a sign up there where we're supposed to turn. It just might say 'Martin's Marsh,' in plain English," Honey suggested. "Let's get started again, before I notice how tired my legs are!"

"Good idea!" Trixie agreed hastily. "Mine are getting a bit wobbly, too. They're sending distress signals to my so-called brain." Trixie groaned as she settled herself again on the bike. "Let's go."

There were no signs pointing the way to Martin's Marsh at the corner of the old Telegraph Road. As a matter of fact, there were no signs of any sort, and, except for two or three lines of tire tracks in the soft, sandy dirt, there was no indication that anyone used the old road. Old telegraph poles, some leaning well out of line, seemed loosely held together by a few slack wires.

There wasn't a hint in the quiet solitude of the spot
that this road, not so long ago, had been a highway from
the river to the rich interior valley. Only a distant hum-
ming gave evidence that, not too far away, a great concrete ribbon of throughway stretched for a hundred
miles, from city to city.

"Well, here we are," Trixie said dismally, "and I suppose that whichever way we decide to go, we'll be going
the wrong way."

But Honey, off her bike now, was standing in the
middle of the road and sniffing the air with a rapturous
expression. "M-m-m! I smell violets! Let's stop right
here and pick some."

Trixie tilted her pert nose and sniffed. "Smells more
like swamp to me," she said flatly. Then, a moment later,
her blue eyes sparkled. "Swamp! Wait a minute!" She ran
to stand beside Honey. "Let's see which way it's coming
from, and we'll know which direction to go!"

"Oh, Trixie, you're a genius!" Honey exclaimed.

They both stood still and sniffed inquiringly. It took
Trixie only a moment to make up her mind. "Nothing
from the east," she announced, then sniffed inquiringly
toward the west. "There! That's it! West!"

Honey wrinkled her pretty nose and pointed it west.
"You're right! Let's go!" she laughed.

A moment later they were on their way.

Honey called over to Trixie as they rode, "Can you
remember any of the landmarks on the map?"

"Golly, I don't think so," Trixie admitted mournfully.
But a couple of minutes later, as they turned a corner,
she gave a sudden exclamation and pointed ahead. "Look!

A big oak split by lightning. Wasn't there something about that on the map?"

"Oak—lightning—why, of course! Now I remember!" Honey agreed excitedly. "Brian drew a tree with a big zigzag of lightning hitting it. There was a road beyond it just a little way, I think, where we turn off."

"Let's take a look," Trixie said eagerly and was on her way before she had finished speaking. Honey was not far behind her as they reached the big oak and went on to look for the turnoff road.

The smell of the marsh was getting stronger every second, and the road was starting to get rougher and narrower.

Suddenly Trixie let her bike veer across the dirt toward Honey, and they almost collided. Her eyes were fixed on something deep in among the trees at the side of the road. "Honey! Look! A huge old house!"

They stopped and stared. At first sight it had seemed like a whole house, one that a person could live in. But a closer look showed that it was only a shell. Three stories high, with part of its gambrel roof still covering the upper story, it stood in the midst of tall trees and a vast tangle of vegetation.

"Reminds me of the Frayne house after Jim's good-for-nothing stepfather accidentally set fire to it," Trixie said. "Fire can really wreck a place, even when it's brick and stone."

"It seems a shame," Honey sighed, "a waste of money. I suppose that's the old Martin mansion where the partner of Captain Kidd lived."

"Dad said that people only suspected that he was

Kidd's partner." Then Trixie added, "But I bet he was,
all right. All sorts of things could have gone on in a spot
that must have been at least a day's journey from the
city. And the Hudson is only a short distance away.
There's a swamp to hide in, besides."

Honey stole a quick look at Trixie as her friend was
speaking. Trixie was getting the look that showed she
was beginning to make plans. "Trixie Belden, you can
just forget it," she said, shaking a finger at her. "I know
what you're thinking."

"Huh?" Trixie looked surprised, and then she laughed.
"We could just take a *little* bit of a look around in there.
You know, I've heard about old places like that having
secret passages underneath, especially when something
unlawful was going on, like pirating. Suppose we just
happened to find a trapdoor or a secret panel, and there
was a tunnel, and—" Trixie's vivid imagination had gone
to work.

Honey interrupted hastily. "And cobwebs and spiders
and rats and maybe—" she gulped—"maybe skeletons.
Ugh! You're not going to talk me into exploring that
house!"

Trixie sighed. "Okay, scaredy-cat. But it would be fun
to look around outside. Maybe we could even find some
antique doorknobs or stuff like that and sell it to make
some money for the B.W.G. treasury!"

Honey looked at her gravely. "You know you're just
making that up. If there had been anything like that
left, after a big fire that did as much damage as this one
did, it would have been taken years ago. But if you
simply must go exploring, I'll go with you."

"I knew you would! Come on; let's wheel our bikes in as far as we can and walk the rest of the way." She started off almost at once, and Honey followed up a narrow driveway almost overgrown with weeds.

The weeds in their path were not half as tall as they would be later in the season, and they could see well ahead, so there was little danger of suddenly encountering a snake. Overhead, brown squirrels chattered angrily at them from the branches, and birds swooped low over their heads, as if trying to scare them away from the newly filled nests. There was a chorus of twitters, chirps, and indignant songs going on all around them.

"Any minute now, that blue jay is going to land right on my head!" Trixie called back to Honey. "She missed me by inches that time!"

Now they were close to the big ruined house. It rose high above the tallest of the trees that had once marked the borders of the formal sunken garden. A tangle of vines, reaching almost three stories high, softened the blackened outlines of windows.

The two girls stood together and looked upward at the fresh green that stretched across the empty windows.

"Can't you imagine old Ezarach Martin up there with his spyglass, looking out over the trees toward the Hudson, watching for Captain Kidd's longboat to bring the loot from some hidden cove down the river?" Trixie spoke softly, as if someone might be up there listening.

Honey stirred uneasily. "I don't think he could see as far as the river," she said. As Trixie suddenly looked thoughtful and started around toward the rear of the house, Honey called after her, "But you don't have to climb up there and find out. Please, Trixie, let's go back to the road now."

But Trixie had disappeared around the corner of the house, and a moment later Honey heard her calling excitedly, "Honey! Come look at what I've found!"

With her heart in her mouth, Honey ran as quickly as she could.

Trixie was peering over a broken wall into a small plot of ground at the rear of the big house.

"What is it?" Honey called as she ran.

"A rose garden!" Trixie said, turning wide blue eyes to her friend.

Honey slowed down to a walk, disappointed. "Oh, is that all? Gosh, Trix, you've seen dozens of rose gardens. What's so remarkable about this one?"

"This one is being taken care of," Trixie told her.

"How can it be," Honey asked, "when nobody lives here? And why should somebody who doesn't live here come and take care of a rose garden?"

"I dunno," Trixie admitted, "but you just take a look yourself."

Honey came and peered over the wall. The rose garden was very old. The main branches of the rose-bushes were thick and spiny, but every one of the bushes was neatly trimmed, and the ground around them had been carefully weeded and neatly raked. "That's strange," Honey murmured. Then she saw Trixie lean over suddenly and study something in the soil. "What have you found now?"

"Footprints," Trixie told her. "Small ones. Anyhow, smaller than *my* feet." She set her foot down beside the print. "Probably a little boy's."

"But they're pointed. Boys don't wear pointed-toed shoes. It's a girl."

"And they've been made since last night's rain," Trixie decided. "Maybe we scared her away." She straightened up and stared all around, hoping to catch a glimpse of the mysterious gardener.

"Trixie, I think we'd better get out of here. We're really trespassing, you know." Honey clutched Trixie's arm nervously and looked about. "Whoever has been taking care of this garden may come after us with a shotgun if she sees us snooping!"

"Huh!" Trixie's eye measured the small footprint again. "Nobody would be silly enough to let a little girl have a shotgun." She frowned. "Wonder why she comes here?"

"Maybe her people have a trailer back in the woods somewhere. Dad says he's seen lots of campers around lately. It's the spring weather that brings them."

"But why should she work around a garden that doesn't belong to her?" Trixie persisted.

"Maybe she happens to like roses," Honey guessed.

"But they won't bloom for another month or so," Trixie objected. "If her people are just camping, they'll probably be gone by then. It's certainly mysterious."

"Well, we aren't getting any nearer to the swamp while we stand here guessing about her. Hadn't we better go look for those flowers and plants we set out to get for Miss Bennett?" Honey asked matter-of-factly.

"Right, as usual," Trixie said cheerfully. "Let's be on our merry way."

But they were due for another surprise. They had

pedaled along the lonely road for only a few hundred
feet, when they went around a bend and found themselves practically in front of another house.

This house stood, small and neat, behind a white-
washed picket fence. And it quite obviously was occu-
pied, for the brick walk to the front door was swept
clean, and the plots of bright-colored spring flowers
were carefully set out and well cared for. Tall maples
stood stiffly like soldiers along either side of the walk.

"How darling!" Honey said, slowing down to admire
the cottage. "Look at the spring beauties. Don't you
love them, Trix? They're such a heavenly shade of pink."

But Trixie, who had stopped also, was more interested
in taking a close look at the letter box that stood on its
pedestal at one side of the gate. Much to her disappoint-
ment, there was no name on the metal box, only a
number.

"Isn't it the cutest ever?" Honey asked with an admiring sigh. "I always wanted to live in a cottage just
like this!"

"Not me," said her more practical-minded friend.
"That well back there near the barn looks as if it were
very much in use even today! The tin cup is shiny, and
the bucket is still wet from being dipped. I'll take my
plumbing up-to-date!"

"But it's so—so charming and—away from things."

"You said it. Too far away," Trixie retorted with a
grimace. "But the well reminds me that I'm awfully
thirsty. Why don't we go in and knock and ask politely
if we may have a drink of water?"

"I'm sure it would be all right," Honey agreed.

They carefully propped their bikes against a roadside tree and opened the gate. It squeaked loudly, startling them both into giggles.

"There's nothing like announcing yourself with a squeaky gate." Trixie grinned, but the grin disappeared a second later. She gripped Honey's arm and held her back. "Look at the window!" she said in a strange voice.

Honey looked and felt a little shiver go down her spine. A bony hand was gesturing from between the curtains of the window next to the door. And, quite unmistakably, the hand was warning them to go.

Then, as they stood staring, wide-eyed, the hand disappeared, and for a flash they saw a small white face with wide-set dark eyes, framed by smooth white hair parted in the middle. Then the face disappeared into the shadows of the room, and the curtains fell.

Without a word, both girls turned and fled through the gate. It took all of Trixie's courage to stop long enough to latch the gate after them and leave it as they had found it.

Then she hurried after Honey to their bikes. Mounting quickly, they pedaled off as fast as they could go, without so much as a backward glance.

Martin's Marsh • 6

It was another quarter of a mile to the edge of the swamp, but Trixie and Honey kept pedaling hard until they came to the broken fence that marked the edge of soft ground.

Trixie glanced back before she braked her bike to a stop, but the cottage was no longer in view. "This looks like it!" she called to Honey, who was close behind her.

Honey wobbled to a stop, dismounted, and sank down on the grass under a white-blossomed dogwood tree. "Thank goodness! I was about to collapse!"

Trixie threw herself down beside Honey, groaning. "I couldn't have gone much farther!" she admitted.

Honey laughed suddenly. Trixie looked at her in surprise. "Now what's so funny?" Trixie demanded.

"Us!" Honey gave a giggle. "Getting panicky and running as if a pack of wolves were after us! Why did we do such a silly thing?"

"I was scared," Trixie admitted a bit sheepishly. She

clasped her knees and rested her chin on them. "I suppose it was that spooky hand waving us away and then that white face staring at us—just staring!"

Honey nodded. "It *was* weird. All I wanted to do was to get away as fast as I could. I was all shivery."

"Now I suppose she'll think we had guilty consciences because we had come to steal her flowers! Maybe we should go back and explain that all we wanted was a drink of water."

"Not me!" Honey assured her promptly. "I got over being thirsty."

"I suppose the little girl who tends the rosebushes lives there with the old lady," Trixie said suddenly. "It's close enough. And maybe the old lady likes roses, and her dear little granddaughter brings them to her in June, and—" Trixie was off on a flight of fancy.

"And we'll still be here in June ourselves if we don't get busy looking for wood sorrel and spearmint and the rest of those plants Brian wrote on the map."

"The only one I remember is tansy," Trixie said with a grin, "and that's because I remember a very old herb book of my grandmother's that had a recipe for tansy cakes that were eaten at Easter."

"Wonder what they tasted like." Honey grimaced.

"Bitter, sort of," Trixie told her. "At least, I think that's what it said. They were taken as a tonic. And the fresh tansy leaves were soaked in buttermilk for nine days, and then the buttermilk was used to bleach freckles."

"Ugh! I'd rather have the freckles." Honey laughed.

Trixie sighed. "That's what you think, because you don't happen to have any." Trixie's freckles, though not

nearly so numerous as Mart's, were a great annoyance
to her. Moms always told her they would disappear when
she was a little older, and Dad said he thought they were
cute, but Trixie had her doubts about both opinions.

"Anyhow, we'll gather some violets. I can see oodles of
them from here. And look, over there in the distance,
aren't those blue flags?" Honey pointed eagerly.

"And I see some yellow lady's slippers over that way."
Trixie nodded in the other direction. She got to her feet
and extended a hand to Honey. "Come on, and bring
the trowel and the basket from your bike. We'll get
samples of all of them and then have lunch."

And a moment later they were picking their way
carefully along a faint path that seemed to lead along
the very edge of the swamp.

But the splashes of color were somewhat farther in
than they had seemed from the edge of the swamp. And
even when Trixie and Honey reached them and began to
choose the strongest and most beautiful of the flowering
plants, they saw still others, deeper in the swamp, that
promised to be much more spectacular. So they continued
to follow a winding path for quite a distance, always
led on by the distant sight of more beautiful specimens.

They both had muddy feet, and the wire basket they
had brought was heaped high with many kinds of plants
before they decided to stop and check over what they
had found.

"I love these bloodroots," Honey said. "Do you know
that they close when the sun sets and that they're very
delicate, in spite of their big leaves?"

"Miss Bennett says the Indians used the red sap of

the bloodroot to decorate their faces and tomahawks."
Trixie carefully enclosed the wet plant with its fragile
white flower in a length of plastic wrapping material
that would keep it fresh until they could get the specimen safely into water at home.

They worked busily for a few minutes and soon had
all the specimens neatly stowed away in the wire basket.

It was a longer hike back to their bikes than they
had realized, and Trixie hurried Honey along. She had
noticed that the sky overhead was getting dark and the
clouds were scurrying past over the tops of the tall trees
that ringed the marsh.

"Let's eat some lunch and then get started home," she
suggested when they were back at the edge of the
swamp. "It's going to sprinkle, I'm afraid."

The lunch that Mrs. Belden had packed was full of
pleasant surprises, and the girls did full justice to it,
down to the last stuffed date and rosy-cheeked apple.

Trixie snapped the lid down on the empty basket and
moaned. "I'm simply stuffed. I know I'll never pedal all
that way home now."

"Why don't we walk our bikes partway, till the fried
chicken is settled down for the ride?" Honey laughed.

Before Trixie could reply, a light spatter of rain
answered for her.

They mounted their bikes and headed for home, but
the sprinkle turned into a steady spring rain before they
had even reached the small white cottage.

Trixie, with rain streaming down her face, called to
Honey, "Why don't we stop at the old witch's house and
ask her to let us come in till the shower's over?"

"I'd rather keep going," Honey called back, with a shiver.

"I know, you're afraid she'll turn us into gingerbread dolls! Or is that the way the story goes in 'Hansel and Gretel'?" Trixie was never sure of her facts about fairy tales.

Honey laughed. "Worse than that! She fattened 'em up and ate 'em. It was her house that was gingerbread!"

They both stared hard at the small cottage as they went past, but no one came to the window. The door of the small barn in the rear was partly open, as it had been when they first went by, but there was no one in sight.

Trixie was riding ahead now, against pelting rain. She stared suddenly at something lying partly in the ditch a few yards beyond the last pickets of the white fence. The object was a small child's bicycle. It was lying on its side and half covered with muddy water as the rain splashed down on it. But in spite of the mud and water that hid it, Trixie could see that it wasn't a rusty old machine that somebody had discarded but a shiny, almost new one.

"Pretty careless," she reflected, riding on through the pelting rain. And she thought with a shudder of what Moms and Dad would say to her or the boys if they treated their bicycles like that. All four had them, and because they knew that their father had paid a good price for the bikes, they were careful of them.

Honey caught up with her, and they rode side by side on the slippery, muddy road. She called over to Trixie, "Did you see the bike in the ditch back there?"

Trixie nodded vigorously. "I guess it belongs to the

little girl who takes care of the rose garden," she said. "She ought to be spanked."

"It was a boy's bike, I'm sure," Honey informed her.

"Then either she rides a boy's bike or she's a he, even if she or he wears pointed shoes," Trixie laughed. "I hope whichever one it is didn't hurt himself-herself when he-she fell into that ditch!"

"Maybe we should go back and see if there's anything we can do, like going for a doctor."

Trixie hesitated, then grinned over at Honey. "That was a pretty neat little cottage. Maybe they even have one of them there newfangled things called tellyphones!"

Honey giggled. "You would have to be sensible when I wanted to be a hero-een!"

So they rode on through the rain and were glad to turn back into Glen Road a few minutes later. Even though Glen Road was called a country road, it was well surfaced, and they no longer had to plow through inches of mud. They pedaled along as fast as they could.

They had almost reached the foot of the Wheeler driveway, when someone close behind them tooted an auto horn loudly. It scared Honey so that she nearly fell off her bike and into the path of the car. Brakes squealed, and Brian, at the wheel of his jalopy, barely managed to stop it a few feet from the wobbling bicycle.

Brian climbed out and ran to Honey as she dismounted unsteadily. Mart, in the front seat, sat looking scared and sheepish as Jim swung out of the rear seat and rushed to his adopted sister.

"Gosh, I'm sorry, Honey!" Brian exclaimed. "My moron brother, here, thought he was being funny!"

"I—I didn't mean to—" Mart's face was crimson as he climbed out of the car and came to them. "I was just—"

"Just being a clown, which comes natural!" Trixie snapped angrily. "Don't bother apologizing. We know that little children must play!"

"Aw, Trix!" Mart mumbled.

"Oh, stop making a fuss," Honey said, laughing. "I didn't take a tumble, did I? That's pretty good for a gal who didn't know one end of a bicycle from the other at one time!"

"It wasn't his fault you didn't fall!" Trixie cast a withering glance at Mart.

Jim decided it was time to change the subject. He nodded toward the specimen basket on the front of Trixie's bike. "I see you girls were a bit more successful in your expedition than we were in ours. We were rained out before we had half the corn planted."

"We have some beautiful specimens," Honey told him proudly. "Miss Bennett will be delighted."

But Trixie was still frowning in Mart's direction. All she said was "Hmph."

Brian caught Jim's eye and shrugged. Jim tried again. "By the way, Trix, I didn't notice till you were out of sight this morning that I'd forgotten to give you back the map. I suppose you came back and found it where I pinned it on the door of the clubhouse."

"Why, no," Trixie said, surprised. "We didn't miss it till we were almost halfway to the swamp and had to decide which way to turn. But we muddled along somehow and finally found the swamp without it."

"Then the map's still hanging there, I guess." Brian

laughed. "And here I flattered myself that you two just couldn't get along without my artistic help!"

"It was a lovely map, and it did help!" Honey smiled warmly at Brian. "We remembered things you had on it, and they helped a lot."

"Good!" Brian was pleased. "And now, Miss Trixie, I'll load your bike on the back of my car, and you can ride the rest of the way home with us. Then, if you like, I'll help you prepare those specimens the way Miss Bennett likes them for class."

"Thanks!" Trixie said, with a sigh of relief. "At least I have one male relative who's not a complete idiot!"

"Only half a one, I suppose!" Brian laughed.

"I didn't mean any such—" Trixie began, but she stopped abruptly as they all heard the low warning whine of a police car siren coming along Glen Road from the direction of town.

A moment later a Sleepyside Police Department car came speeding into view, its red light busily blinking.

Everyone jumped back, to be well out of the way when it passed, but, to their amazement, it slowed down at the foot of the driveway, then swung in and went up the drive to the front of the mansion.

Trixie was the quickest to react. "Something's wrong!" she exclaimed.

Honey turned white and looked as if she might be going to faint. "Mom—Dad—oh!" she whispered, clutching Jim's arm and swaying.

"Whoa!" Jim started to laugh, and his arm went across his sister's shoulders. "Somebody probably telephoned headquarters that there was going to be a party for our small celebrity tonight, and they're here to find out if we need a detective to guard the guests' jewels."

"A party? Oh!" Trixie's blue eyes brightened.

"For the Arts Club ladies to meet Gaye and her aunt." Jim grinned. "Which means I stay in my room and study!"

"I couldn't have attended the party, anyhow," Trixie said, putting on a society-matron air. "I'll be much too busy. I do hope poor Gaye won't pine away when I don't arrive."

Jim chuckled. "Small chance! Not after she came back looking for you two and I had to explain that you had decided to go on without her. I told her you were sorry, but it didn't help."

"She *did* have to practice, didn't she?" Honey asked uneasily. "I'd feel awful if I thought my mistake made us hurt her feelings."

"I'll say she had to practice!" Jim assured her. "Her loving aunt marched down to the clubhouse personally and dragged her, weeping, to the practice dungeon."

Mart leaned against the car and snickered. "Weeping? Yowling like a banshee, you told me, friend. As I recollect, you said she yelled louder than Bobby with soap in both eyes!"

Even Trixie had to laugh, to Mart's relief. It meant that she wasn't angry any longer. Mart always felt better when he and Trixie were on good terms, though it was almost always his fault when they squabbled.

"I suppose I should go tell her I'm sorry," Trixie said grumpily.

"We'll give her a bunch of those yellow violets and a couple of the extra blue flags," Honey suggested. "You know, as a tribute to her genius or something."

"Great!" Trixie giggled. "She'll eat it up!"

"Women!" Brian said with a sad shake of his head and a side wink at Jim.

Jim grinned in reply, but before he could add his comment to Brian's, they all noticed a tall, broad-shouldered figure hurrying toward them down the driveway. It was Regan, the head groom. Regan was the friend and confidant of all of them and, when it came to stable behavior and duties, their boss. He was always good-natured, except when one of them became a bit slack in grooming a horse or was careless taking care of the gear.

Regan's broad smile was missing as he came up to them. "Glad I found all of you before you broke up," he said in an unusually serious voice. "Sergeant Rooney wants to talk to you up at the house."

"Goodness! Why?" Trixie asked in surprise.

"Because he hopes one of you can give him a lead on where Miss Gaye has disappeared to!"

Missing · 7

GAYE? GONE?" Honey gasped, her hazel eyes wide with shocked surprise.

"Looks like it," the groom answered soberly. "We've just about turned the place upside down looking for her and that little white pooch of hers. No luck."

"She's probably hiding," Trixie suggested quickly.

But Regan shook his head. "Don't know where. That clubhouse of yours is locked, isn't it?"

Jim spoke up. "I'm the last one who left there this morning, and I tried the door before I turned away."

Regan was disappointed. "Well, that's about the last hope we had—the clubhouse. I guess we'd better mosey up to the house and let the sergeant talk to you kids."

Jim, Mart, and Brian walked ahead with Regan, while Honey and Trixie brought up the rear. There was an uneasy silence between the two girls until the others had gone beyond hearing distance. Then Honey, with a worried frown puckering her brow, said, "I hope she didn't go far into our woods. There's the lake, you know."

"Hmph!" Trixie wrinkled her small nose. "She's probably a champion swimmer. The lake wouldn't be big enough for her to condescend to go swimming in it!"

"I suppose she does know how to swim, at that," Honey agreed, relieved.

"What *I* think is that she's hiding under the bed to worry her aunt, if she was as angry as Jim says she was when she got dragged away to practice."

"Or in a closet in one of the guest bedrooms," Honey suggested.

"Wherever she is, I'm sure she'll show up for dinner!" Trixie predicted lightly.

"But I wonder why they sent for the police." Honey looked worried.

They were in front of the huge Wheeler mansion now, and the boys were waiting on the steps for them.

Mart met them with a grin. "You dolls be sure to clam up," he hissed, pulling at an imaginary moustache. "Don't let on we've got her bound and gagged in the old ice-house."

They both giggled, and Trixie pushed Mart out of the way as they hurried up the steps after Regan.

Sergeant Rooney of the Sleepyside Police satisfied himself that none of them could throw any light on the whereabouts of the famous young violinist. He was very much inclined, Trixie guessed from his offhand manner, to think that this was all much ado about nothing.

Miss Trask, the Wheelers' efficient housekeeper, had assured him that no one belonging to the household had seen the child since midmorning.

Honey's mother had been in her room resting all day and could add nothing to that.

Trixie and Honey told a straightforward story about their expedition to the marsh. "We knew Gaye had to practice," Trixie said, "so we didn't wait for her to come with us."

Miss Crandall, mopping tears from her eyes, admitted that she had had a slight disagreement with her niece about practicing. "Nothing serious, of course," she assured the officers. "The dear child is high-strung, like all great talents. A little firm discipline now and then is the only answer." Her lips made a thin line as she concluded, and Trixie felt suddenly sorry for Gaye, wherever she was. Moms was right, she reflected. Gaye *did* lead a different kind of life from hers and Honey's. And it couldn't be a very happy one, with stern Miss Crandall in charge.

"And you've searched every room?" Sergeant Rooney asked Miss Trask, while his young officer solemnly made notes in a small black book.

"Oh, yes," Miss Trask assured him firmly, "and every possible hiding place around the house. I'm afraid the child has run away."

"Officer, you must find her before some terrible accident happens to my dear little niece!" Miss Crandall clutched at Sergeant Rooney's arm. "She's not used to being out all alone in the dark." Her voice broke.

Sergeant Rooney eyed her suspiciously. Trixie could see that he wasn't impressed by Miss Crandall's emotion. "It's still a long way from being dark, Miss Crandall. I'm sure she'll turn up safe before you have anything to worry about." He chuckled. "Most runaway kids dash home quick when it comes around to the next mealtime!"

Miss Crandall frowned. "I hope you're right, but my niece is no ordinary child. If she should meet with an accident that would injure her hands, her career would be ruined. You must find her at once!"

Trixie nudged Mart and whispered indignantly, "She sounds as if that *career* is all that matters!"

"Shh!" he whispered. "Can't you see she's concealing her trepidation behind a false facade of insouciance?"

Trixie snorted. "Whatever that's supposed to mean, I don't believe it! And I bet you can't even spell insou— whatever it is!"

"I'll just take you up on that—" Mart started, but he broke off to scowl toward the doorway. "Now, how did the *Sleepyside Sun* find out what was going on?"

The butler was admitting Paul Trent at the front door and showing him to a chair in the foyer. Paul was carrying a manila envelope.

"Looks like he brought those pictures they took yesterday," Trixie guessed. "Gaye's aunt has to okay them."

"Oh, that's right," Mart agreed. "For a minute there, I thought he might be a mind reader!"

They grinned at each other. "Not after watching him quarterback Central High last year!" Trixie laughed.

Miss Crandall was wringing her hands and moaning, "Somebody must find her! Can't anyone do anything?"

Mart felt a smart tap on his shoulder and turned hastily to see Paul Trent close behind him. "What's going on, sonny? Who's missing?" Trent asked importantly.

Trixie suppressed a giggle as she saw Mart flush. If there was one thing that Mart disliked nearly as much as being called Trixie's "twin," it was being called "sonny."

"Why don't you ask the law over there?" Mart snapped.

Trent scowled at him. "You're one of those smart-aleck Bob-Whites, aren't you? From that crummy Sleepyside High?" He sneered and started to turn away.

"Yeah, that 'crummy' school that walloped you thirty-eight to three last term!" Mart gave an insulting little snicker. "Boy, I'll bet Central was glad when you graduated!"

Trent's sneer turned to a scowl, and his fists doubled as he towered over Mart. Trixie interrupted hurriedly. "It's little Gaye. She's run away somewhere."

"Gaye? Jeepers!" Trent forgot Mart at once and abruptly dashed off to talk to Sergeant Rooney.

Mart glowered after him. "I should have smacked him! What did you have to speak up for?"

"To keep you from getting a punch in the nose!" Trixie told him. "So thank me." But Mart only scowled.

Trent's voice came through a sudden hush. "It looks like a kidnapping to me, Sergeant. They'll probably get a ransom note any minute."

Mitzi, Gaye's maid, shrieked, and Miss Crandall promptly toppled over in a faint and would have fallen if the sergeant hadn't moved quickly to catch her. He led her to a chair and left her in the weeping Mitzi's hands before he marched back to confront young Trent.

"Where did you get that nonsense about kidnapping?" he demanded brusquely.

Trent scowled and looked uneasy. An audible snicker from Mart did nothing to help. Trent flashed Mart an angry look and then asked Sergeant Rooney sullenly, "How do you know it's nonsense? The kid makes a fortune with her fiddle. Why wouldn't some crook get the idea of a kidnapping?"

The sergeant said coldly, "There's no evidence of such a thing. I don't know where you got the idea," he said, glancing toward Mart and Trixie and their fellow Bob-Whites before he continued, "but wherever it came from, forget it till we find something that points to it." He frowned. "Clear?"

The young reporter nodded and looked crestfallen as the sergeant and his assisting officer moved away, quietly discussing the case.

Miss Crandall was moaning as she recovered from her faint, and Gaye's governess and the maid were hovering over her, nervously getting into each other's way as they ministered to her.

Sergeant Rooney stopped by the solemn-faced little group of Bob-Whites. "I want all of you to try to think where the youngster may be hiding. You know, some old play spot of your own, a cave or an old building here on the estate."

"Regan and the chauffeur have looked just about everywhere imaginable and had no luck," Jim explained gravely.

The sergeant nodded. "I know. But one of you might know some special place."

"We'll try to think," Trixie promised.

"Good." Sergeant Rooney nodded. "The sooner we find her the better. Kids sometimes get themselves in a jam playing runaway." He started after his assistant

officer but stopped and looked back at them with a grim
little smile. "But, for the love of pete, don't start any
wild rumors about kidnap plots. There's nothing to point
to any such thing."

"If that dumb reporter Trent says we gave him that
goofy kidnap idea, he's lying," Mart told him quickly,
with a scowl.

"That's right, Sergeant," Trixie added quietly.

Sergeant Rooney nodded. "Trent didn't accuse you
of it. It was just a little suspicion that came to me, and
I'm glad it wasn't so."

After the sergeant and his assistant had driven back
to town to report, an uneasy silence settled down at the
Wheelers'. Miss Crandall retired to her suite to check
over the photographic proofs with a very subdued Paul
Trent. He had, as Mart, grinning, confided to Brian and
the girls, lost most of the wind out of his sails after the
sergeant's rebuke.

The Bob-Whites stood in a group until Jim, looking
thoughtful, said, "Seems as if we ought to be doing
something about Gaye, but we'd better wait until there's
a real reason to worry. Sergeant Rooney's probably right."
The other four nodded.

Mart and Brian walked down to the foot of the driveway with the girls, while Jim went to catch up on some
of his load of senior homework. He was taking two extra
subjects, preparing for his entrance into college in the
fall, and every spare minute of his time had to be used
for study.

While the boys were loading Trixie's bike into the
car for the short ride home, Honey solemnly promised

to phone Trixie the moment there was any news about Gaye. "I wish we could go looking for her together around here, but Mom has several things she wants me to do to get ready for the party tonight."

Trixie nodded, with a glum expression. "If there *is* a party. It would be just like that little imp to hide somewhere till morning, just to spite her aunt!"

"I hope she has more consideration for Mom and the Arts Club than to do a stunt like that!" Honey's hazel eyes flashed. "Mom and her committee have worked hard getting people to buy tickets for the recital, and they've been counting on this party to help boost the sale."

Brian and Mart had lifted Trixie's bike into the car and were ready to start for home. Brian started to climb into the driver's seat. "Come on, Trix. Plenty to do at home, from the looks of this bundle of junk you brought from the marsh."

"Okay, be right with you," Trixie called. "Don't forget to call," she reminded Honey hastily.

"Don't worry. I'll phone the moment she shows up," Honey assured her. Then, with a cheerful good-bye to the boys, Honey trundled her bike up toward the stable.

Trixie stopped as she was about to enter the car and looked toward the clubhouse door. "You know," she told Brian, "Gaye could be in there hiding. Even if the door *is* locked, she could have squeezed in through that side window if one of us left it unlatched."

"That's an idea," Brian agreed. "I'll take a look." He strode up the walk to the door as Trixie and Mart watched, then went around out of sight at the side of the vine-covered cottage to examine the window.

But a moment later he reappeared, shaking his head. "Window's locked," he reported, starting to rejoin them. He changed his mind suddenly and turned back to try the door. It, too, was locked, and he turned away again.

"Bring our map while you're at it," Trixie called. "Jim pinned it to the door."

But the map was not pinned to the door. Nor was it anywhere in sight on the ground nearby.

Trixie hurried to help look for it, while Mart waited impatiently.

"It probably blew away, and somebody picked it up and put it in the trash can," he suggested.

"Golly! I hope they didn't!" Trixie wailed. "I wanted to show it to Miss Bennett and the class on Monday. It was such a lovely map, with those cute drawings of yours, Brian."

"Well, thank you, small sister! Your praise is music to my ears, or something!" Brian laughed.

"Huh!" Mart remarked dryly. "She didn't think it was such a masterpiece when she dashed off and forgot it this morning!"

Trixie gave him a withering look, but Brian merely grinned. "Never mind, Trix, I'll do you another and really let my artistic ability show."

"Brian, you're absolutely the darlingest—" Trixie beamed at her big brother.

"Sap," Mart said, finishing her sentence for her. Then, as she glared at him, he strolled back to the car. "Come on. It's gone, so why worry?"

But Trixie had noticed a tiny piece of paper in the

tall grass beside the walk, and she made a sudden swoop to recover it. "Here's part of it!" she exclaimed. "The pin's still in it."

"Let's see." Brian took it from her fingers. "The pin is bent, as if someone had jerked at the map before the paper tore. I used heavy paper so it wouldn't go to pieces if you kids got it wet while you were wandering around in the marsh, trying to match my sketches with the plants there."

"Then it didn't blow away, after all," Trixie said, frowning. "Somebody deliberately tore it down."

"A tramp, probably," Brian suggested. "Or some kid biking past and just plain curious. I hope he didn't decide it was a treasure map and try to follow it!"

"He'll end up with wet feet if he did!" Trixie laughed. But as she climbed into the rear seat of the jalopy a few minutes later and they started for home, she sobered suddenly at a thought. There was one person who might have been very interested in that map: Gaye!

Gaye could have hurried back to the clubhouse when she escaped from the music room and her practice session. Finding the map pinned to the door, she could easily have recognized it as the one that the girls had intended to use on their flower picking excursion.

Perhaps she had decided to use it to follow them to the marsh and prove to them that she could find her way.

But Gaye would have had to walk, probably carrying Mr. Poo, whose delicate little feet could never have taken him several miles. But then, even though Honey and she had stopped for lunch and spent a long time picking the swamp plants, Gaye could hardly have reached the marsh on foot before they had come pedaling out on their way home. They would have been sure to meet her on the road.

Gaye could have caught a ride as far as the marsh, however, and wandered in looking for them while they were at the other end. The rain could have sent her into some shelter off the road. In that case, perhaps she was still there—lost and frightened.

Trixie wondered if she ought to tell the boys what she was thinking. Maybe they would decide to turn the car around and drive out to the marsh to search. But even as she leaned forward to interrupt their discussion of fuel injection and initial acceleration, whatever that was, she sank back again.

After all, *anybody* could have come along and taken the map. She hadn't a shred of evidence that it had been Gaye. It would be better to wait to say anything until she arrived home and found out if Honey had phoned any news about the missing child.

She sat silent, until Mart turned suddenly and stared at her in mock surprise. "Hey! Where's that brilliant outburst of chatter we customarily receive from our feminine sibling?"

"Oh, let me alone," Trixie retorted. "Can't you see I'm quietly getting an education by listening to your brainy conversation?"

They were just turning into the Belden driveway.

Brian stopped the car with a flourish and a roar of his engine. "All ashore that's going ashore!" he sang out cheerfully. "Crabapple Farm, last stop!"

Mart hopped out and started unloading Trixie's bike.

"Come on; come on; look alive!" he barked as Trixie took her time getting out of the car. "Climb out of the barge, Cleopatra! I can't hold this thing all day!" He let go of the bike, and it started to wobble crazily down the driveway.

Trixie moved fast to catch it before it could crash. "Thanks, dear," she said sarcastically. "You have such *pretty* manners. Pretty awful, I mean!"

And while Mart, pink-cheeked, was trying to think of a fitting retort, she marched her bike up to the garage storeroom, where all the Belden bikes were kept in a neat row.

It wasn't until she had put her own bike in its regular rack that she noticed that Bobby's bike wasn't there. That was unusual. Dad had made it a firm rule that every bike had to be put away safely after being used. Bobby knew that as well as the rest of them did, and he always obeyed.

"Yikes! I hope Bobby hasn't left it standing out somewhere! Moms will be furious with him. I guess I'd better look for it and put it away for him," she decided quickly.

She started out of the storeroom but saw Brian carrying an armful of the plants she and Honey had gathered at the swamp. He would expect her, of course, to lend a helping hand in getting them ready for Miss Bennett on Monday morning. After all, it was *her* project, and he was just being obliging.

But, in spite of her good intentions, she ducked back out of sight till he had passed. "I'll help him as soon as I find Bobby's bike and put it away," she told herself. "Though I'm sure Brian will do a much neater job alone."

She dashed about, trying to find the half-size bike, but it was nowhere in the yard or the orchard.

When she did get around to the potting shed, Brian was just labeling the last bunch of the plants.

"About time you showed up, Lady Jane," he growled.

"I'm sorry, Brian," she said contritely. "I intended to come sooner, but I had something important to tend to, really."

"Forget it, fuzzy head!" Brian said good-naturedly, tousling the short curls on top of her head. "I didn't mind doing it by myself."

"You're an angel! And thanks millions!" Trixie grinned happily at him, blowing him a kiss. "I just know you're going to be the best doctor in the whole world someday, because you never mind doing things for people." Before Brian could get over his embarrassment and find an answer, she had darted off to look for her mother.

Her mother was reading and resting as Trixie came into the cheerful living room. Saturday afternoon was her time to relax, with Bobby safely asleep and dinner preparation still a couple of hours off.

"Has Honey phoned any news, Moms?" Trixie asked.

"No, dear, but I just spoke to Miss Trask. There's still no sign of that little rascal Gaye. Miss Trask feels sure that the child is deliberately hiding to worry Miss Crandall about her performance at the party for the Arts Club tonight. She feels sure Gaye will put in an appearance any moment now, especially since it's getting close to Mr. Poo's dinner hour, and Gaye loves him too much to let him be hungry."

"She's a funny little thing," Trixie said soberly. "I wish

I could like her. I'm trying, Moms, really, but I'm not doing so well, I'm afraid."

"You will, dear," Mrs. Belden told her serenely.

But Trixie was not so sure. Her sigh said as much. She helped herself to an apple and munched it thoughtfully, strolling across the room and back restlessly.

"Is there anything you need me for here?" she asked finally.

"Not for a couple of hours." Her mother smiled as she answered. She studied Trixie a minute and then put down her book. "There's something on your mind. Don't you want to tell me what it is, dear?"

Trixie hesitated. Then she asked suddenly, "Moms, did Bobby get the signed photo from Gaye this morning?"

Her mother looked surprised. "Why, no, dear, he didn't. As a matter of fact, he rode his bike over to Wheelers' right after breakfast, hoping she'd have it all ready for him. And when he got there, she was already practicing that concerto or sonata or whatever it is that she is doing tonight for the Arts Club. She wasn't allowed to stop to come down and talk to him. I think that was part of the argument she had with her aunt just before she disappeared."

"I'll bet Bobby was terribly disappointed," said Trixie. "I was hoping that maybe he'd seen her and could tell us if she'd mentioned running away."

Mrs. Belden shook her head. "No, he didn't see her at all. And to top it, something went wrong with his bicycle brake, and Regan wouldn't let him start for home again on it. He made Bobby leave it for him to fix this afternoon."

Trixie was suddenly tense. "Then Bobby's bike is over there?"

Her mother frowned, puzzled. "Why, of course. It was very good of Regan to offer to fix it, even though Bobby wasn't too happy about having to walk home." She shuddered. "I'm only thankful that nothing broke while Bobby was riding. He might have ended up in a muddy ditch, with a bruised knee or a skinned nose—or worse!"

Trixie's eyes widened suddenly with excitement. "Oh!" she said in a small voice.

Moms had opened her book again. She looked up in surprise. "Oh, what?" she asked quickly.

"Oh, nothing, Moms," Trixie assured her hastily. She had decided not to say anything about the sudden thought that had come to her mind at mention of the muddy ditch. That small bicycle in a muddy ditch out near the strange old lady's house—that could have been Bobby's! Gaye could have found it and used it! And that would answer the question of how Gaye could have reached the swamp and disappeared while the two girls were still gathering the plants deep in the marshland. But if she did—what had happened to her after that?

"Moms, please," she said abruptly, "may I go and see if Regan's fixed Bobby's bike? If he has, I'll bring it home so Bobby can ride in the park with me tomorrow after Sunday school."

"Go ahead, dear." Mrs. Belden's eyes twinkled. "It's very thoughtful of you. Besides, I wouldn't think of keeping you here while all the excitement is going on over there. But be back in a couple of hours, so we can start getting dinner ready and eat on time."

"Thanks, Moms! You're wonderful!" Trixie dashed for the door, and a moment later she was running down the driveway.

A Piece of Glass · 8

REGAN WAS BUSY around the stable as Trixie came hurrying up the Wheeler driveway.

"Hi," she called breathlessly to the tall groom. "Any sign of Gaye?"

"Not yet," Regan answered soberly.

"Do you think she might be hiding around here somewhere?"

Regan looked thoughtful. "I did at first," he admitted, "but I'm not so sure now. Miss Crandall is fit to be tied because we haven't found her, but I don't know of a place on this whole property, including the lake, that we haven't checked. It's getting to look like that half-baked reporter kid hit the nail on the head when he guessed it might be a kidnapping."

"Golly, I hope not!" Trixie breathed. "Are there any clues?"

Regan shook his head. "Nope. But that might not mean anything. A gang of professional crooks would be too smart to leave clues." He picked up a pitchfork and started into the stable.

Trixie called after him, "Moms was wondering if you'd had time to fix Bobby's bike. I can wheel it home if it's ready."

Regan turned with a look of chagrin on his honest face. "I knew there was something I was forgetting. Drat it! I've been running in circles all day."

"That's okay, Regan," Trixie said quickly. "I can take it the way it is, and Brian can probably fix it in the morning."

Regan hesitated. "Well," he said finally, "I hate to go back on my promises, Trixie, but maybe that would be better, after all. When I finish here, I've got to take another walk around the lake to the boathouse, just to make sure we didn't overlook any signs there."

Trixie nodded and asked hopefully, "Could I go along and look, too?"

The stableman shook his head emphatically. "No, thanks. Just run on up to the toolshed. It's open. Be sure to tell your mom I'm sorry I didn't get around to fixing the bike. And tell Brian the brake probably only needs tightening."

"Okay, and thanks, anyhow," Trixie called back as she started up the long, winding driveway.

As she trudged up toward the toolshed, she couldn't help feeling a little disappointed. Here she had been so sure that Gaye had taken the disabled bicycle and ridden to the marsh. And all the time, the bike was safe in the toolshed. A fine detective she was!

As she pushed open the toolshed door and looked

inside, her heart beat faster again. There was no bicycle there!

Then there was still a good chance that Gaye was out at the marsh, she thought excitedly. She simply had to get out there and examine that muddy bike in the ditch. If it *was* Bobby's, she could rush back with the news, and they would soon locate Gaye.

Trixie glanced at her wristwatch. In a little more than an hour and a half, Moms would be expecting her back to help prepare dinner. How could she get out to the marsh and back again in that short space of time?

She heard Lady whinnying down at the stable. The little thoroughbred was Mrs. Wheeler's pet, but she had been too busy lately to exercise her regularly, so Regan had taken on that job in addition to all his regular duties. Sometimes he let Trixie take Lady out instead of steady old Susie, but a lecture always went with it, plus warnings to take good care of the part-Arabian Lady.

Trixie made up her mind suddenly. She started running down the driveway, calling, "Regan!" as she saw Regan and young Tom Delanoy, the chauffeur, coming out of the stable leading Lady.

Regan turned a surprised face toward her and waited for her breathless arrival. "Now what? I thought you went to get Bobby's bike," he said good-naturedly.

She gave a careless wave of her hand. "It can wait. Please, Regan, may I exercise Lady this afternoon? I haven't had a ride today, and I'd just love it."

"Well, now," Regan beamed, "it would be a help, right enough. Don't go too far or too fast, and don't slack on the grooming if I'm not here when you get back."

"Don't worry; I'll be careful," Trixie promised.

Two minutes later, she was on her way at a slow trot. But once she was beyond reach of Regan's eagle eye, she put Lady to a faster pace and was soon cantering along.

Luckily, there was little traffic on Glen Road on a Saturday afternoon, and she covered ground rapidly. Almost before she realized it, she had reached the turn-off beyond the lightning-struck oak tree. And soon she was in sight of the small neat cottage near the marsh.

There was no sign of the old woman at the window, and the barn door was still partly closed.

Trixie dismounted hurriedly and dragged the bicycle free of the mud that had half covered it. There was no mistaking it. The metal nameplate that Brian had attached to the frame was still in place.

She knew that she had guessed right. Gaye had found the bike and ridden off on it, probably carrying the little poodle on her arm or in the wire basket. She had ridden safely this far, only to lose control and end up in the muddy ditch. Where Gaye had gone after that was something Trixie made up her mind to find out as soon as possible.

"Let's see, now," she asked herself, "where do you think *you* would have gone first? Why, that's simple. Right over to the cottage, to get warm and dry!"

She left the bicycle leaning against a tree to dry off, and she tied Lady to a low branch of the same tree. "Take care of the bike, old girl," she told Lady, scratching the mare's soft nose. "And rest, because something tells me you're going to have quite a load going home!"

The gate squeaked loudly, just as it had earlier when she and Honey had started into the neat little yard. But this time there was no spectral hand at the window, waving her away.

Trixie knocked on the door, timidly at first, and then with more force. There was no answer.

Her heart sank. Her hopeful thought that she'd find Gaye here didn't seem to be true. Maybe the child had wandered toward the swamp instead. She could have fallen hard back there in the ditch and hurt her head. Or Mr. Poo the poodle could have run away when the bike fell, and she could have run after him into the swamp.

Trixie tried again, knocking more loudly. But when there was still no answer, she turned away, wondering what to do, which way to look. Then she heard the sharp, shrill bark.

She felt sure it was Mr. Poo barking. He had sounded just like that yesterday in the orchard.

The sound was not coming from inside the cottage. It seemed muffled now, but there was no mistaking that it was from somewhere not far away.

Trixie hurried away from the door and rounded the corner of the cottage. Surprisingly, the barn door was closed tightly now. And as she stared at it, frowning, she heard a faint bark from that direction.

Trixie stalked over and pushed open the barn door. Inside, it was too dark for her to see anything at first. She stood on the threshold and stared in, feeling a small shiver down her spine. Finally she gathered courage and stepped inside.

But she still could see nothing but darkness and smell only ancient leather and musty hay.

"Gaye?" she called, her voice making echoes. "Are you in here? It's me, Trixie Belden, Gaye! I've come to take you home."

There was no answer from the shadowy depths of the barn. A faint light from a dust-and-cobweb-covered window high in the loft failed to show any details of what lay ahead. Trixie stood her ground in spite of an impulse to run.

"Gaye!" she exclaimed impatiently, her voice breaking in spite of her. "I know you're here! Answer me right now!"

But there was only silence. If Gaye was there, she had no intention of answering.

But if Gaye wouldn't answer, perhaps the poodle puppy would. Trixie stuck two fingers into her mouth and gave a shrill whistle. While it still echoed, she called, "Here, Mr. Poo! Come get a nice big bone!" The mention of a bone always brought Reddy. But apparently bones were not on the elegant dog's diet. There was no answering bark.

Trixie stepped farther into the barn, well out of the patch of sunlight that had followed her inside. Now she could see the outline of an old-fashioned buggy against the far wall. Above it, a shallow loft stretched the width of the barn. A rickety ladder, minus a lower rung, leaned against the loft. Up there, Trixie could make out the ends of a couple of leather trunks and some barrels piled against the side wall. Musty hay swayed in the breeze from the open door behind Trixie.

"She could be hiding up there," Trixie thought, but she dismissed the idea as she moved closer and saw the cobwebs that were everywhere. "Not our delicate little Miss Gaye of the concert stage," she told herself. "A spider would panic her!" Trixie heard a sudden small rustle in one of the stalls. She tiptoed over and popped around the corner of the partition, expecting to find Gaye and the little dog hiding there.

Instead, something white rose up out of the musty hay and flew at her, wings flapping wildly.

Trixie gave a shriek and ducked out of the way as an old setting hen flew past her, clucking loudly, and took a perch high in the rafters.

Trixie expected to hear a giggle, but there wasn't a sound. Suddenly it seemed very spooky in the old barn. Trixie turned around and fled out into the pale spring sunshine, closing the door hastily behind her.

She went slowly around toward the front of the cottage. Two things she knew: It was Bobby's bike in the ditch, and the missing child was the only one who could have left it there. The mystery was where Gaye had gone.

And it *had* been Mr. Poo's hysterical bark she had heard. She had heard enough of it yesterday afternoon not to forget it so soon. But it hadn't seemed to come from inside the house. Maybe she had decided that mistakenly. Perhaps he was in a back room and the windows were closed. That would make his bark sound far away.

For the first time she felt a little shiver of fear. The thought came back to her that maybe Gaye had been hurt badly when she fell off the bike. That could have been why there had been no answer to her knock a few minutes ago. Maybe the old lady had gone for a doctor.

Trixie made up her mind to get inside and find out.

She hurried to the front door again. This time she fairly pounded on the door. "I'll wait two minutes, and if I don't get an answer then, I'm going to try the door. I don't care if it is illegal to walk into people's houses without being invited. I've got a very good reason, and I'm sure I couldn't be arrested."

But this time, no sooner had she pounded on the heavy oak door than she heard light steps coming from beyond the door.

"Gaye," she thought. "She must have decided to show herself."

But it was not Gaye who flung the door open and stood facing her with an angry frown. It was a wiry little old lady with white hair parted in the middle. And the face was the one that had stared out at her and Honey from between parted curtains this morning.

Trixie was so startled that for a moment she couldn't speak.

The little old lady snapped angrily, "Who are you and what do you want? Can't you take a hint when a person doesn't answer the door when you knock? And what were you doing prowling around in my barn, young lady?"

"I—I'm sorry." Trixie found her tongue. "I was looking for a friend of mine."

"Well, don't look for him around here. This is private property."

"It isn't a him. It's a her," Trixie said hurriedly. "A

little girl with long yellow curls. She plays the violin."

"I don't care if she plays the harp and carries it around with her!" the old lady said firmly. "She hasn't been here, and I'm not expecting her. So run along!" And with that she stepped back and slammed the door in Trixie's face.

Trixie's face was red. "Thanks for being so polite!"

Then she turned and stalked down the brick pathway toward the small white gate.

As she leaned down to unlatch the gate, she noticed something shining up from between two bricks in the walk.

It was glassy and seemed to flash when the sunlight struck it.

"Piece of bottle," Trixie decided. But she leaned over and picked up the shiny object, anyway.

To her surprise, it was cut like a gem. It was about the size of the diamond that Honey and she had found in the gatehouse floor months ago. Had she found another?

She let it lie on her palm and reflect the sunlight. "If it's anything valuable, I ought to take it to the door and give it to the old meanie," she thought. But just as she decided to do it, she turned the stone over and saw that it was a piece of glass with colored backing painted on, like the rhinestones that Moms had sewed on her costume when she was eleven and played the fairy queen in the school play. Just a rhinestone, but quite a big one.

She started to flip it into the grass, then stopped suddenly. She had seen a lot of rhinestones like this lately.

They were decorating something. What was it?

All at once she remembered. That silly collar of Mr. Poo's was set with rows of glittering fake diamonds like this. It was the first thing she noticed when the little dog leaped at Reddy yesterday afternoon.

Finding the piece of glass here meant that he and Gaye had been inside the gate. And if they had been inside, they could both be in the cottage with the strange old lady, in spite of what she said.

But why hadn't she admitted Gaye was there? It was very strange.

Trixie had to know if Gaye was inside the cottage. But how could she find out? She was sure the old lady wouldn't answer her knock again, no matter how long she might hammer on the door.

For once, Trixie had to admit to herself that it was too much to figure out alone. She knew that she needed help.

"Bob-Whites to the Rescue" • 9

TRIXIE DROPPED the shining rhinestone into her jacket pocket and went out through the squeaky gate. She tried her best not to seem in a hurry. She felt sure that the old lady was watching her through the window again. And, unless she was wrong in her guess, Gaye was probably right beside the old lady, giggling because she knew that she was worrying everyone by hiding. By riding away slowly, Trixie hoped she could give them the impression that she had given up looking for Gaye there.

If Gaye were to suspect that Trixie intended to come back again with somebody to help her search, the little girl would probably hide in the swamp with Mr. Poo till she was certain that everyone was worried sick about what had happened to her.

So Trixie strolled over to Lady and climbed into the saddle without looking back toward the house. She rode at a walk at first, but as soon as she had gone around the first turn, she slapped Lady smartly on the flank and urged her into a brisk canter.

"I guess I'd better go right on up to the house and tell Miss Crandall what I've found out. I mean, what I *think* I've found out." She didn't know what Miss Crandall would want to do. Maybe she'd want to go right out there and find out if Gaye really was in the cottage, or she might prefer to call the police and let them go. But it seemed to Trixie, just then, that Miss Crandall was the person she should talk to first.

She was over halfway home when she remembered that she had solemnly promised Regan that she wouldn't run Lady. She hated to slow down now, but she had to. If Regan suspected that she had disobeyed orders, she'd be grounded for a week. So she slowed the mare to a trot the rest of the way.

It seemed ages before she reached the foot of the Manor House driveway. She saw that there were still a couple of cars in front of the big house. One of them looked like the rental car that Paul Trent was using. He was probably hanging around with his tongue out for the news in case anyone found Gaye. Trixie wished that she had been able to bring Gaye home with her from the marsh cottage. That would have shown Mr. Trent that the Bob-Whites *did* know a few answers.

She was passing the little clubhouse when she noticed that the door was standing ajar. She wondered who could be in there. If that Trent character was snooping around inside, she made up her mind, she'd tell him off, but good, especially after his mean crack about the club members.

But when she pushed the door open all the way, the person she saw was Jim Frayne. He was surrounded by books and papers and was concentrating so hard on studying that he didn't know she was there.

Trixie felt guilty at interrupting him, and she started moving backward quietly, pulling the door closed after her. Unfortunately for her good intentions, she caught one heel against a bit of uneven planking and tripped, falling flat on her back with a dull thud.

Red-faced, she scrambled to her feet at once and saw Jim standing in the doorway, looking surprised.

"Now what are you up to?" he demanded with a grin. "That's no way for a lady to come calling on a gent."

"I wasn't coming; I was g-going," Trixie told him indignantly, her face getting redder. "I was b-backing away so I wouldn't interrupt your studying."

"Where have you been?" Jim took a keen look at the waiting mare. "Lady looks beat. You haven't been running her, I hope. Regan will skin you alive."

"Does she look that bad? I slowed her down a long way back." Trixie's blue eyes were troubled.

Jim studied her a moment. "What were you running from, Trix?" he asked soberly. "Did somebody bother you?"

"Oh, no! Nothing like that," she assured Jim hastily. And then she suddenly made up her mind to tell him about the house by the marsh. "It was just that I was in a hurry to get here. I've been to Martin's Marsh, and I think I've found out where Gaye is!"

"Gaye? Oh, great!" Jim's whole face lit up. "Where?"

"Out there, in a cottage near the marsh. Or I'm pretty

sure she is!" Trixie told him eagerly. "I was on my way to tell Miss Crandall."

"Wait a minute," Jim said gravely. "You say you're pretty sure. You're not just guessing?"

"Well, partly guessing. But I found Bobby's bike there, in a ditch, and I'm almost certain Gaye rode it there. And I found *this* on the brick walk." She handed him the rhinestone with the painted back. "I think it fell out of her dog's collar."

Jim studied the rhinestone, without speaking.

"Don't you see? Gaye *must* be there! There's a scary old woman living in the cottage who says she never saw Gaye, but I don't believe her. And I'm sure I heard Mr. Poo barking in the house."

"You say you're *pretty* sure, *almost* certain, and *think* this thing could have fallen out of the poodle's collar— but you're not really sure of anything except that somebody took Bobby's bike and left it in a ditch. Isn't that so?"

"I suppose it is," Trixie admitted honestly. "It could have been the old lady's dog I heard. But it seems to me Gaye *could* be there."

"If you tell Miss Crandall, she'll hit the ceiling and want to go charging out to the marsh place with a bunch of cops." Jim looked troubled. "And Gaye may not be anywhere near there."

"I know." Trixie nodded. "But we can't just let *nothing* happen, in case she *is* there!"

A car was turning into the driveway. It was Brian's jalopy. He saw them and brought the car to a stop. "So there you are!" He sounded cross. "Where's that bike of

Bobby's you were supposed to bring home?" He shook
his head reproachfully at his sister. "The little imp woke
up from his nap half an hour ago and has been yowling
ever since that he wants to take a ride on his bike."

"I'm sorry—" Trixie began, but Brian interrupted.

"I had to give him my stopwatch to play with to keep
him quiet, and I suppose there'll be nothing left of it
by the time I get back! If he wrecks it, I'll sue you! Now,
where's the bike?"

"Against a tree out near Martin's Marsh," Trixie said,
"and I think it was Gaye who left it nearby."

"Gaye? Now, wait a minute. What is this? Gaye out
at Martin's Marsh? You're kidding!"

"No, she isn't," Jim told him seriously. "There's a good
chance Trixie found the answer to Gaye's disappearance.
The question before the house now is what we'd better
do about it."

"Fill me in." Brian turned to Trixie.

It took only a couple of minutes for her to tell Brian
about the mysterious cottage at the marsh. He looked
grave as she finished.

"What do you think she should do? Tell Miss Crandall
or phone the police?" Jim asked.

"I'd say don't do either until you have a lot more
evidence than Trixie has found so far," Brian said
promptly. "I happen to know that the old lady who lives
in the cottage out there is very respectable. In fact, she's
the last of the Martins, Miss Rachel. She's lived in that
cottage ever since the big Martin place burned forty
years ago. Dad knows her. He's had to go out there
several times on business for the bank."

"But she acted so weird!" Trixie protested.

"People who live alone get pretty set in their ways," Jim told her with a smile. "Maybe you interrupted her daily beauty nap."

"But what about the rhinestone from Mr. Poo's collar? How do you think that got there?" Trixie persisted.

"You don't know for sure that it *is* from his collar," Jim reminded her. "I guess we do have a pretty shaky case."

"Then aren't we going to do anything about it?" she asked indignantly.

The two boys exchanged uneasy glances. "How about dashing out there in the car and getting the bike?" Brian suggested. "We can be back before dark if we just take a quick look around. We might be able to pick up a trail if the kid wandered into the swamp instead of going to the cottage."

"I want to go with you," Trixie said.

"What about Lady? Are you going to let her stand there and catch cold?" Brian asked. "I think you'd better get her up to the stable and start grooming her, before she gets chilled."

"Gleeps! I almost forgot her," Trixie moaned.

Brian looked inquiringly at Jim, and Jim nodded. "Okay," Brian agreed, "you've nagged us into it. We'll help you with Lady, and then you can come with us."

The stable seemed deserted as they led the mare in and went to work on her.

It took only a few minutes for Brian and Jim to clean the tack with saddle soap and sponge while Trixie was brushing Lady. She wasn't quite finished with the job

when they put the top on the saddle soap can and
squeezed the sponge dry.

"Come on, slowpoke!" Brian teased her, and when
she threatened to throw the brush at him, he took it
from her, and he and Jim finished grooming Lady while
Trixie stood off and bossed the job.

Then, while Brian took Lady to her stall and made
her comfortable, Jim carried the saddle into the tack
room. Trixie followed with the brushes, soap, sponge,
and currycomb.

"Trix," Jim said suddenly as he turned from hanging
up the saddle, "don't you think you'd better let Brian
and me go out alone to Martin's Marsh? I don't want to
scare you, but—well, you know, all sorts of accidents
happen to people in swamps. And if Gaye is hurt—"

Trixie shook her head. "I'll be all right. And I'm still
just as sure as anything that she didn't wander into the
swamp. It must have been raining when she fell into
that ditch, and I'm positive she wouldn't have gone anywhere except to Miss Martin's cottage. She *must* be
there!"

"I hope you're right." Jim was very solemn. "Well,
come on; let's get started. We haven't much daylight
left."

He hurried out, and Trixie took a couple of steps
after him. As she did, something cast a moving shadow
across the window, and she distinctly heard a footstep
on the gravel along the side of the building.

She crossed the room quickly, unfastened the window
screen, pushed it up so she could poke her head out, and
looked up and down the length of the walk behind the

stable. But there was no one in sight. Whoever had passed the window just now was gone, down one of the alleys between the buildings.

She withdrew her head quickly and fastened the screen securely. Then she hurried out to tell the boys that someone might have heard their plans to go out to Martin's Marsh to look for Gaye.

Jim and Brian refused to get excited about it. "It was probably one of the assistant grooms or Mike the gardener. He keeps his new mower in the end building because there isn't room for it in the toolshed. It's one of those big ones with a seat for the guy who's running it," Jim said. "He's promised to let me run it next time he barbers the grass. It ought to be a kick."

"Say, how about letting me try it? That old elephant of Dad's has me worn out from pushing it around our two bits' worth of lawn," Brian told him. "Let me know when you'll be piloting it."

Trixie looked from one to the other, and her eyes flashed. "Maybe it wasn't the gardener, after all, but somebody who was spying on us!" she said loudly, to get their attention. It was annoying how they got all excited about a silly old lawnmower and refused to worry about important things.

"Oh, sure!" Brian teased her. "It was probably Miss Rachel Martin herself, disguised in a long white beard. Come on, let's get this over with and bring that bike back to our howling baby brother before he drives Moms wild!"

They each took an arm and hurried Trixie down to the waiting jalopy.

"In you go, duchess," Jim said, ushering Trixie into the rear seat. "Bob-Whites to the rescue!"

Brian climbed in and took his place at the wheel, and Jim got in beside him. "Lead on, Macduff," Jim said, with a sweep of his arm.

"It isn't 'Lead on, Macduff,' at all," Trixie told him crossly. "It's 'Lay on, Macduff,' and it's from *Macbeth*."

"Oh, no! Now she's going literary on us! I never thought it could happen." Brian groaned as he put the car in motion and headed toward Glen Road.

But Trixie glanced back up the driveway as they turned into the road and was almost certain that the figure she saw come out of the stable and stand staring after them was Paul Trent.

She wondered if she should mention it to the boys. They were already deep in a discussion of things called camshafts and tappets and other weird-sounding names that she guessed were parts of the jalopy. She decided not to mention Paul Trent.

Even if the person she had seen near the stable had been Paul, it was perfectly natural for him to be there, since he was probably questioning everybody, hoping to get some kind of scoop about Gaye for his newspaper. She didn't like him, but, after all, it was his job.

And there was nothing to connect him with the mysterious person who had passed the tack room window and disappeared. Jim was probably right that it was only the gardener or one of the grooms.

So she sat silent while Brian drove swiftly along Glen Road and took the turnoff into the old road that led to Martin's Marsh.

Miss Rachel • 10

THE OLD ROAD was still muddy and slippery from the noontime rain, and Brian had to slow down his small car as they neared the marsh road.

"Can't we go any faster?" Trixie complained, after a glance at the rapidly sinking sun. "We don't want to be wandering around here after dark."

"Cheer up, Sis," Brian called back to her. "There's a good half hour of light left. If we can't find Gaye in that time, we might as well give up and go home. We'll know that your hunch misfired."

"I don't see why you keep calling it a hunch," Trixie flung at him crossly. "If *you* had found Bobby's bike in the ditch and all the rest of the clues, you'd call it evidence, I'm sure."

"Hold everything, kids," Jim chuckled. "We'll soon know what to call it. I see what must be the ruins of the old Martin mansion off there to the right. The cottage should be close now."

"It's just around the next bend. We'll be there in half a sec," Trixie told him. But at that moment, the small car went into a skid, and she added hastily, "That is, if we ever do get there!" and closed her eyes.

Brian hung tightly to the wheel and braked with short, sharp jabs until the car was under control. It had turned almost completely around, but it hadn't hit any of the big trees alongside the road. He carefully guided it back to the proper side of the road. "Phew!" he said as he stopped it. "That was a pretty close one!"

"Neat work, sonny," Jim told him lightly.

Trixie opened her eyes and unclenched her fists. "Are we all here?" she asked with an unsteady grin. "Never a dull moment. It's a good thing days like this don't happen often. I simply couldn't stand the strain!" She pretended to fan herself with her hand.

"Hoity-toity, madam," Brian jeered. "You faint, and we make you walk the rest of the way!"

They were passing the ruins a moment later, when Trixie bounced up suddenly. "Those footprints were Rachel Martin's. They must have been!"

Brian groaned. "Now it's footprints! I was wondering when she'd find some footprints! The gal is footprint dizzy!"

Jim was more serious. "What footprints, Trix?"

"The ones Honey and I saw in the rose garden back of the ruins of the Martin place. They had pointed toes, and we couldn't decide if a little boy or a girl had left them. Now I remember that Miss Rachel Martin was wearing old-fashioned buttoned shoes with pointed toes when she talked to me at the door. So it's only logical that the footprints must have been hers!"

"Logical, my small sister, but quite irrelevant. What does it prove about Gaye's whereabouts?" Brian teased.

Trixie hesitated, and Jim grinned at her. "Got you there, Miss Belden!"

Trixie frowned at them and tilted her nose. "Well, anyhow, it's interesting," she said loftily and lapsed into silence until they had turned the corner and were in sight of the small white cottage.

Brian stopped the car close to where the bike stood against the tree near the muddy ditch.

"There!" Trixie said triumphantly, pointing to it.

"I don't hear any barking," Jim said, getting out.

"Mr. Poo is probably asleep," Trixie guessed.

"I hope we don't interrupt his dear little nap," Brian chuckled. "That is, if he *is* here."

"Let's get the bike loaded into the car before we go to the cottage," Jim suggested.

It took the two boys only a few minutes to drag the small bicycle out of the mud and load it into the backseat of the car.

Trixie watched silently, casting uneasy glances toward the cottage. She expected to see Miss Rachel come stalking out at any moment to order them away.

The sun was now a ball of fire behind the tall evergreens beyond the cottage. In a few minutes it would dip down and be gone. Then there would be only a short period of spring twilight before dark settled down. They would have to hurry if they had to go on to the swamp to look for Gaye.

"Well, who faces the lady dragon in yon castle?" Jim

asked as he closed the car door. "Let's pick a victim."

"She won't even open the door if she sees it's me back again," Trixie said promptly, "so it's got to be one of *you.*"

"Ungrammatical, but possibly true," Jim agreed, with a wink at Brian. "So, Dr. Brian, polish up your best bedside manner and try it out on the lady."

"Oh, see here, now—" Jim's kidding had gotten Brian a little flustered.

"Duty calls." Jim grinned. "Scoot along, Doc."

Brian snorted, "Chicken, hey?" And as Jim pretended to take a swing at him, Brian ducked and laughed.

"Do hurry," Trixie said, with a nervous glance at the disappearing sun. And Brian, sobering suddenly, walked rapidly toward the cottage.

Jim and Trixie watched for a moment as he went in at the gate and hurried to the door. Then Jim glanced toward the barn. "Did you look carefully inside there?" he asked.

"As well as I could," Trixie told him, "but it was so dark and cobwebby, I felt sure Gaye would never hide in there." She shuddered. "At least, *I* never would!"

Jim nodded. "I hid in a place like that once, when I was running away from my stepfather. It was scary after dark, with the funny noises and mysterious shadows."

"Ugh!" Trixie shivered.

"Hey! The bedside manner is working!" Jim nodded toward the cottage. Trixie stared. Brian was talking to Miss Rachel, and there was a pleasant smile on the face of the little old lady in her old-fashioned starched cotton dress. She held out her hand to Brian in a friendly greeting, and a moment later they both turned toward Trixie and Jim.

"Hey, Trix! You and Jim come here. Miss Martin wants to meet you."

"Well, what do you know?" Trixie's jaw dropped.

"Good old Doc Belden scores again!" Jim laughed, and he took her arm as they hurried over to join Brian at the cottage door. Miss Martin waited for them with a smile.

"There hasn't been any little girl here except yourself," she told Trixie pleasantly. "I'm sorry I was so short with you this noon, child. I didn't know then that you were Peter Belden's daughter. You Beldens have lived in Sleepyside almost as long as we Martins have been here. Your father is a fine man."

"Why, thanks, Miss Martin." Trixie beamed.

"My sister is sure she heard Gaye's poodle barking somewhere around here earlier," Brian said with a smile. "You may have seen him. A small white puppy. Gaye took him with her, we think, when she ran away."

Miss Rachel shook her head. "I haven't seen *him*, either."

Trixie glanced past the elderly woman, still hoping to·see some evidence that Gaye was there. But the neat, small living room showed nothing except that Miss Rachel was an excellent housekeeper and owned some fine furniture.

"Well, I guess we'd better head for the swamp right away. That's probably where she went, after all," Jim said gravely.

"The swamp? Oh!" There was a sharp edge in Miss Rachel's voice. "Do be careful, all of you, if you try to look for her there! It's a terrible place!"

"That's the reason we've got to hurry, Miss Martin," Trixie said quickly. "If she's lost in there, she might fall into a hole or something."

"Yes, I know!" Miss Martin cast a frightened look in the direction of the marshland. "Oh, do hurry before it gets really dark. Others—" Miss Martin's voice grew suddenly so soft it was almost a whisper—"others have been lost in there." She stared off, with a shiver.

"We're on our way right now," Brian said hurriedly. "And thanks!" He motioned Jim and Trixie to follow him as he turned away. Trixie hesitated and tried to think of something polite to say, but Miss Martin was still looking off, with a strange expression on her face, so, after a moment, Trixie turned and followed Jim and Brian down the narrow brick walk toward the gate.

"I wonder why she's lived here so long, when she's so afraid of the swamp. *I* wouldn't," Trixie stated flatly as she caught up with the boys. She spoke softly, because Miss Martin was still standing in the doorway.

"Maybe when the old family mansion burned down, she had no other place to go," Jim guessed quietly. "I imagine that this cottage was the servants' quarters originally."

"Uh-huh." Brian nodded, but he was frowning. "I suppose so. I was trying to remember something Dad told me about the Martins one day after he'd been out here on bank business. He said there'd been some kind of family tragedy a long while ago—about the same time that the big Martin place burned down."

"Let's ask him about it tonight," Trixie said quickly.

From a long way off they heard the sound of a car siren. "Hey, listen!" Jim said suddenly. "Police!"

"Chasing a speed bug on the highway, probably," Brian guessed. "Sound carries a lot farther at night."

Both boys stopped to listen, but Trixie plucked at her brother's sleeve. "Come on, Brian. Let's go to the swamp. Can't you see how dark it's getting? If Gaye finds herself alone in there in the dark. . . ." She gulped as her voice trailed off.

But she didn't have to finish. They knew what could happen.

They started through the gate but stopped suddenly as the police car siren became louder.

"Headed this way." Jim frowned. "That's strange!"

"Did you tell anyone about Bobby's bike?" Brian asked hastily.

"Only the two of you," Trixie assured him. Then she remembered something. "Oh! That reporter from the *Sun!*"

"What about him?" Brian scowled.

"I saw somebody watching us from the stable just as we drove away from Wheelers', and I'm sure it was Paul Trent. And the person who was sneaking around outside the tack room could have been Trent, too. He could have phoned the police and told them where we were coming to look for Gaye."

Headlights came into sight at that moment, and they saw the blinker light of a police car. It slowed down as it came up.

"We'll know in a minute," Jim said quietly as they stood waiting.

"Look! I knew it!" Trixie exclaimed indignantly. The first person to jump out of the police car was Paul Trent. He saw them and came swaggering over.

"Did you find her?" he called out importantly.

Trixie glowered at him and so did Brian. It was Jim who answered casually, "Find whom?"

In the background Miss Crandall was being helped out of the police car by Sergeant Rooney.

"Gaye, of course!" Trent snapped.

"What makes you think we were looking for her here?" Jim asked coldly.

"Why, I heard—I mean—" Trent was stammering as they stared woodenly at him. "That is—uh—"

Trixie stuck her chin out at him. "You mean you sneaked around listening to a private conversation!" she snapped. "Well, it won't do you much good, because she just isn't here!"

Sergeant Rooney and Miss Crandall hurried up to them. "Where's the kid?" he demanded.

"We haven't found her," Brian told him. "Miss Martin says she hasn't seen her around."

The sergeant wheeled on the young reporter. "I thought you claimed they had proof she was out here! What's the idea? Giving false information to the police is a misdemeanor!"

"But I thought—" Trent squirmed unhappily. He broke off under the sergeant's glare. Sergeant Rooney turned his back to the reporter.

"Okay, kids," he said a bit grimly to Trixie and the

two boys. "What's the story?"

Trixie explained in a few words about finding the bicycle in the ditch and why she thought Gaye might have left it there and be somewhere around the old cottage.

"We were just on our way to the swamp to try to find her, when you arrived," Brian added.

The sergeant looked grim. "I'm glad you didn't. There's a lot of dangerous quicksand in there, and some of it is close to the footpath. It's no place to wander after dark."

"I know I'll never see my darling niece again! Oh-h-h!" Miss Crandall leaned on young Trent's shoulder and sobbed.

Trixie had a sudden idea. "Miss Martin might know someone who could guide you through the swamp at night," she told the sergeant. "There she is at the door, watching us."

"Might be a good idea to ask her," the sergeant agreed, and he started up the walk.

Paul Trent called out after him, "While you're at it, you'd be smart to take a look around inside the house. It still could be a kidnap plot, and the kid could be stashed away in some back room and held for ransom!"

Miss Crandall gave a loud moan at the word "ransom," but the sergeant glared disgustedly at Trent. "That tune of yours is getting on my nerves, buster," he snapped. "Forget it! Miss Martin's respectable. Her folks owned half of Westchester County when Indians owned the other part!"

"Okay, okay!" Trent lapsed into sullen silence, but

the look he gave Trixie as she hurried after the sergeant was angry and accusing.

"Why, Officer Rooney!" Miss Rachel put out a frail white hand in greeting to the young policeman. "I haven't seen you since the road went away from here!"

Sergeant Rooney grinned and touched his cap. "It's Sergeant now, ma'am. And I'm sorry to bother you, but we've got to find someone to guide us into the swamp so we can look for that little girl the Beldens told you about."

"The swamp? Tonight?" Miss Rachel's face looked drawn. "Oh, no! It's too dangerous."

Trixie felt a shiver crawl up her spine. Miss Rachel's eyes looked enormous, and, even in the half-light, Trixie could see that she seemed frightened.

Sergeant Rooney spoke soothingly. "Now, Miss Rachel, we'll be careful. Just tell us somebody who can show us through."

But Miss Rachel shook her head firmly. "There's no one. After a hard rain like today's, even the one path that's usually safe would be underwater. You must wait till daylight."

"Too late," the sergeant said grimly. "We'll have to get in there and find her before she panics." He touched his hat and strode back to the police car.

Miss Rachel shook her head as she watched him go.

Trixie said impulsively, "I'm sorry we bothered you, Miss Martin, but you do see how important it is to find Gaye as soon as we can."

"*If* you can," Miss Rachel sighed, with another nervous look toward the swamp. Then as Trixie started to turn away, the elderly woman stopped her. "Did you say the little girl had yellow curls?" she asked thoughtfully.

"Oh, yes." Trixie nodded. "Very pretty golden ones, practically down to her waist."

"Emily's curls were like that, and her hair looked just like spun gold when the sun shone on it," Miss Rachel said. She had a faraway look and spoke almost in a whisper.

Trixie was startled. Emily? Who was Emily? She opened her lips to ask Miss Rachel, but before she could speak, the noise started.

It was coming from inside the barn. Someone was pounding on the closed door. A voice was crying hysterically, "Let me out! Let me out!" and a small dog was barking shrilly.

Trixie recognized that voice, and she knew that sharp little bark.

Gaye and her poodle puppy had been found.

Someone Named Emily · 11

FOR A MOMENT, everyone was too startled to move. Then Sergeant Rooney hurried toward the barn, with Paul Trent, Jim, and Brian close on his heels.

Trixie took a quick glance at Miss Rachel. She wondered if Miss Rachel would show by her expression that she had known all along that Gaye was in the barn. But she saw with relief that Miss Rachel seemed just as surprised as the others.

Now Miss Crandall ran after the men, as Gaye's sobs and yells kept on, to the accompaniment of Mr. Poo's excited barks.

It took Sergeant Rooney only a minute to drag the pin out of the hasp that held the barn door secure, and then he flung open the door. Gaye came stumbling out, followed by the joyfully barking puppy.

Trixie heard Miss Rachel catch her breath suddenly and cry out softly, "Emily!" And when Trixie turned to look at her, the little old lady had buried her face in her hands and was sobbing pathetically.

"Emily again!" Trixie thought, puzzled. She looked back quickly toward Gaye, who was now clasped in Miss Crandall's arms, crying loudly. There was something about Gaye's appearance that didn't seem just right. It puzzled Trixie for a second, until she realized that the child was wearing a frivolous little lace-trimmed white dress made in the style of forty years ago. It was at least a couple of sizes too large for her. Trixie remembered seeing a dress like that on a picture of Aunt Alicia, in a snapshot album in the farmhouse attic.

"Now, how did she get hold of that outfit?" Trixie wondered.

The answer came to her suddenly. The little imp had gotten into one of those old trunks up in the barn loft and helped herself! She had probably been hiding up there while Trixie was searching for her and had deliberately kept quiet, hoping it would worry Trixie.

And now, Trixie thought disgustedly, she was acting for all her worth, looking pathetic as she leaned against her aunt's shoulder and pointed at Miss Rachel accusingly. "She locked me in her barn!" she wailed. "I was scared!"

"Well, you're out now, kid," Paul Trent assured her, with a scowl toward Miss Rachel, "and we'll see she doesn't get her hands on you again!"

That was too much for Trixie. She stormed over to confront Gaye accusingly. The others, even Jim and Brian, looked surprised.

Blue eyes flashing with anger, Trixie told Gaye loudly, "You're just putting it on, Gaye Hunya! I happen to know you were hiding in the barn. And when I came to look for you, you scrunched down in the loft and kept Mr. Poo quiet, so I wouldn't know you were there!"

Gaye pushed Aunt Della's arms away and glared at her accuser. "I hate you!" she yelled. "You ran away and left me, when you promised I could go with you!"

Paul Trent scowled at Trixie. "Let the kid alone. Can't you see she's had a bad time? What are you trying to do?"

"Get her to tell the truth!" Trixie flashed. "Miss Martin didn't lock her in purposely. She didn't even know Gaye was in the barn!"

"She did too!" Gaye shouted, starting to cry again. "You're not telling the truth," Trixie said flatly.

"That's enough, Trixie!" Sergeant Rooney sounded very stern. "I think I'd better have a talk with Miss Martin."

But when he brought Miss Rachel over to them a couple of minutes later, he was at ease.

Gaye was still sniffling and trying to look tragic, but this time the sergeant only smiled at her and then turned to Miss Crandall. "I think we'd better get her back to the Wheelers', Miss Crandall. She's a little mixed up. I think the truth is that she fell asleep in the loft after Trixie went out, and when she woke up, Miss Rachel was locking up for the night. I don't know, Gaye, why you didn't let Miss Rachel know that you were there, unless it was because you had opened one of those trunks that didn't belong to you. Was that it?"

Gaye scowled at him and hung her head. Miss Crandall frowned. "Is that where you got that awful outfit?

Where are your decent clothes?"

Gaye sniffled. She nodded toward the barn and answered meekly, "Up in that balcony or whatever it is. I was wet and cold, and I didn't think anybody would mind if I put on some dry things nobody was using."

"It's all right," Miss Rachel said with a little smile. "I'm glad you could use it, child. And I wish you and your friends would come in for a cup of my hot mint tea. It would warm you all up for your trip home."

"No, thanks," Miss Crandall said stiffly. "As soon as the dress is laundered, Gaye will return it, with her apologies, and pick up her own clothing." She snatched Gaye's hand. "Come along, now. We'll discuss your misbehavior later."

Trixie expected yells from the little girl as Miss Crandall led her away, but Gaye went along meekly.

Trent sullenly watched them go but made no effort to follow them. Sergeant Rooney clapped him on the shoulder good-naturedly. "There goes your big kidnap scare, kid. Spoiled little girl hides for kicks, but, thanks to Miss Trixie here, no harm done!" He beamed at Trixie.

Trent scowled toward Trixie and the boys and spoke loudly enough for them to hear him. "Yeah, Miss Trixie's a smart little cookie. Everybody knows that. I'll see she gets credit. This little stunt could sell a lot of tickets for the Arts Club! Hooray for the Bob-Whites!" Then he laughed and swaggered away toward the car.

Sergeant Rooney chuckled. "He's a bad loser. Don't mind him, Trixie. We don't think you cooked up the whole deal, even if *he* does!" He grinned and added, "Or *says* he does!"

Trixie was bewildered. "I don't understand. That's just silly of him."

Jim scowled. "I think I'll go take that up with him, before he makes any mistakes in his story!" He turned away to follow Trent, with a grim look on his face.

"Hold it," Sergeant Rooney said quickly. "Let him go. He's just spouting off to save face, after all his loud talk about a kidnapping. He doesn't really think Trixie or any of you had anything to do with Gaye's running away."

"He's a nut if he does," Brian growled.

But Trixie wasn't at all convinced that the young reporter was "just spouting off." She thought uneasily that she would feel a lot better after she had seen what the *Sun* had to say in its Monday edition about the affair.

"Too bad the little demon had to get Miss Rachel mixed up in her mischief," Brian said. "She's a sweet old lady."

"I think so, too," Trixie agreed quickly. "Oh, I meant to ask you whether Dad ever mentioned someone called Emily when he talked to you about the Martin family."

"Not that I remember. Why?" Brian seemed surprised.

Trixie explained about Miss Rachel calling out the name when she caught sight of Gaye in the little white dress.

"I just wondered who Emily was," she concluded.

"Dad's sure to know," Brian said. "Why don't you ask him at dinner—*if* we ever do get home before midnight!" He glanced suggestively at his wristwatch.

"Yikes!" Trixie clapped her hands to her head. "Moms will skin me alive! Let's get started this minute! I promised I'd be back in a couple of hours, and here it's already getting dark!"

They piled hurriedly into Brian's jalopy and sped homeward. Jim jumped out at the foot of the Wheeler driveway and vanished in the twilight, with a wave of his hand.

Moms didn't scold. She had been in touch with the Wheelers and knew everything that had been going on.

"I've had expert help," she told Trixie, giving her a peek at Mart, who was glumly setting the dining table. Trixie stifled a giggle as she carefully backed away from the dining room door.

"Just go wash up and see that Bobby's ready for dinner," her mother suggested.

"Okay, Moms!" Trixie dashed off to find Bobby.

"Where's my bike?" he demanded accusingly, when she finally located him watching the baby chicks in the new incubator. "I been waitin' an' waitin', an' I bet you forgot to get it."

"Oh, no, I didn't! It's right in its stall, and in the morning, after Sunday school, you can go riding with me. Won't that be fun? We'll go exploring and pick some wild flowers for Moms!"

"I want Gaye to come, too. I want her to 'splore with us."

Trixie couldn't help feeling a tiny twinge of jealousy again, but she swallowed it and said quickly, "We'll invite her, but she may be busy. You know, Gaye's not an ordinary little girl with lots of time to play with other children."

Bobby frowned. "You don't like her."

"Of course I do!" Trixie assured him. "Now come along and get cleaned up, or Moms will be angry."

Bobby let her take his hand and lead him toward the house. "Gaye's so pretty. I just *love* Gaye. I hope she stays at Honey's house a long, long time. Don't you, Trixie?"

"Oh, sure!" Trixie said hastily. "Let's hurry now."

"Ask her about tomorrow now," Bobby demanded as they came into the house and started upstairs. "Call her."

"I haven't time right now, Bobby," Trixie explained hastily. "I'll call her later."

"But I have to go to bed early," Bobby protested.

"Okay, I'll come wake you up as soon as I talk to Gaye. How's that?"

"Well—" Bobby thought it over—"awright. But don't forget!"

It wasn't until they were about to sit down to dinner that Trixie noticed that Dad's place was not set.

"Where's Dad, Moms? I wanted to ask him something about Miss Martin," Trixie said.

"He ate early and dashed over to Wheelers' to talk about some business or other with Mr. Wheeler. He'll stay on for the reception, and I'll join him as soon as I'm able to."

"I'll be glad to run you over, Moms," Brian said.

"Thanks, dear. I'll phone Miss Trask that she needn't send the car for me, in that case."

"Nice going, bud," Mart said sourly to Brian. "I peel potatoes and scrape carrots, and now I get stuck with the dishes, as well."

"Seems to me there's a certain curly-headed squaw

not more than a mile away from here," Brian said with a meaningful look at Trixie, "who'd be glad to lend you some expert help."

"I wonder where she could be?" Mart asked, pretending to look all around the room and under the table.

"You can stop being silly, both of you. And I can do the dishes without any china-breakers pretending to help me!" And Trixie elevated a snub nose at both her big brothers.

"Ah! But it's a poor job that doesn't need a boss to watch it!" Mart grinned. "So I'll hang around and keep you amused with my witty sallies while you labor."

But a little later, when Brian and their mother had left, Mart and Trixie washed and dried the dishes and forgot all about their little squabble as Trixie told Mart about Gaye and the borrowed white dress that had seemed to startle Miss Rachel.

"I can hardly wait for Dad to get home so I can find out who Emily was," Trixie concluded.

"Ah! A mystery, hey? Well, it's been all of a couple of weeks since we had one kicking around here!" Mart teased.

"You can laugh, but if you'd seen Miss Rachel's face when she saw Gaye, you'd wonder, too!"

Out of the Past · 12

THEY WERE ALMOST finished with the dishes when the phone in the study rang. It was a mad dash, but Trixie got to it first and heard Honey's voice.

"Hi, Honey!" she said, settling down in her father's overstuffed chair, with her feet over the side. "How's it going?"

Mart waved a dishcloth at her from the doorway and melted away back to the kitchen. "Don't talk all night!" he called back and then disappeared.

Honey's voice sounded a little worried. "Gaye's in bed, resting till the last minute before the people start arriving. She looks to Miss Trask as if she might have a fever, but Miss Crandall says it is just that she's so high-strung and so nervous after her shocking experience this afternoon!"

"What she needs is a spank or two," Trixie said with a disgusted snort. "Her aunt must know that she hid up in that loft deliberately when I was trying to find her.

124

If she had answered me, none of the rest of it would have happened."

"I suppose Miss Crandall does know it, and she's probably furious with Gaye." Honey's worried tones turned to a giggle. "Gaye's maid told Miss Trask that Miss Crandall doesn't dare to cross Gaye too often, because Gaye gets even by pretending to be too ill to practice and then has to be coddled and bribed."

"One good thing," Trixie said, laughing, "she won't be able to cause an uproar very much longer. She'll have to leave soon on her tour."

"Thank goodness!" Honey said quickly and then seemed to feel ashamed. "Oh, I shouldn't have said that. I guess we don't realize that it can't be much fun to be a child prodigy."

"I s'pose that's true," Trixie admitted soberly. "Moms says that she's glad there are no prodigies in our house. We're about as far from that as we can get, I guess."

"Who cares?" Honey had her laugh back. "I wouldn't want to live with one, I know. Not if they're all like our dear little Gaye!"

"It would be a shame if she disappointed all those people who have promised to come tonight," Trixie said indignantly.

"It really would," Honey agreed, "especially after Mom and her committee have worked so hard."

"Well, I guess that's how it is with prodigies." Trixie sighed sympathetically.

Mart appeared in the doorway. He had a wedge of blueberry pie in his hand and a rim of blue around his lips. "You can stop stalling here now. I just scrubbed the last of the pans," he said and took another bite.

"Ugh! Excuse me, Honey; I've got to go now," Trixie said into the phone, "but call me again if anything exciting happens." She hung up the receiver and glared at Mart. "I suppose you know that's the last piece of pie!"

"Sad, but true," Mart admitted, gulping another chunk.

"It happens to have been *my* piece," Trixie told him coldly. "I didn't eat it at dinner, because I was saving it for breakfast. And now you're gobbling it!"

"Dear me, I'm so sorry!" Mart grinned with blue teeth. "I only did it to save you from falling a victim to excessive avoirdupois, dear sibling!"

"Hmph!" Trixie snorted scornfully, but a moment later she giggled. Mart had tried to cram the last large bite of pie into his mouth as he finished speaking, but he had dropped half of it on his shirt. "That'll learn yuh to watch your langwidge, podner!" she teased as she started past him into the hall.

"Hey, wait a minute, Trix!" Mart looked with dismay at the mess on his clean white shirt. "Gosh, how can I get this stuff off my shirt? Moms will scalp me! I was supposed to wear it to school Monday."

"Gleeps! You'll start a new style!" Trixie laughed.

"Quit clowning, Sis!" Mart pleaded. "What will take the stain out?"

"Hm-m-m." Trixie pretended to be thinking hard. "Let's see now. Should it be soaked in milk or—no, that's ink stains. Salt and lemon juice? Nope, that's for rust."

"Come on-n!" Mart begged. "Have a heart!" He had

an inspiration. "I'll help you cart those weeds to school Monday morning if you lend me a hand with this mess."

"It's a promise!" Trixie twinkled. "Okay, I remember now! On to the kitchen, double time. March!"

Mart had a little trouble getting the stained shirt off without spreading the gooey stains, but he finally managed it while Trixie was putting on the teakettle.

When the water started to boil, Trixie spread the stained shirt over a large mixing bowl and held it stretched taut. "All right, now," she told Mart, "hold the kettle as high as you can and pour the boiling water through the stain. But don't splatter it on me, or I'll yell so loud old Miss Martin out at the marsh will hear me!"

Mart stood on a chair and tipped the steaming kettle over the bowl.

"It's starting to fade!" Trixie exclaimed excitedly.

"What is this?" Brian's voice came from the doorway. "You witches brewing up a love potion or something?"

"I'm saving his life—not that he deserves it," Trixie answered, and, when Mart had finished pouring the boiling water and had jumped down off the chair, she held up the shirt for Brian to see. "Just like new—if you don't look too closely. Kind of a pale blue shadow." She handed it to Mart. "Hang it on the service porch. If you ask me sweetly in the morning, I'll iron it for you."

"You're reah-lly not a bad sort, sistah deah!" Mart held an imaginary monocle to his eyes. "Thanks awf'ly!"

"You two!" Brian chuckled.

"Anything going on over at Wheelers' yet?" Trixie asked, perching on the end of the kitchen table and swinging her legs as she bit into an apple.

"People are starting to arrive. And I caught a glimpse of the little fairy princess watching from the window when I let Moms out at the front entrance."

"I hope that means she's going to perform. Honey said she was still jittery after this afternoon, according to Miss Trask."

"I wouldn't know. I just dropped Moms, had a little gab with Dad, and dashed on back." Brian chose an apple for himself and leaned against the table beside Trixie as Mart came back in from the service porch.

"I hope Dad and Moms come home before I have to go to bed," Trixie told Brian. "I'm dying to ask Dad if he knows who Emily could be."

"*Was* is the word," Brian said calmly.

"Brian! You found out! Who was she?" Trixie demanded eagerly.

"Rachel Martin's little sister. She was drowned in the swamp the night that the Martin mansion burned down."

"Oh, my goodness!" Trixie's blue eyes were like saucers. "Go on!"

"It was a pretty awful thing, Dad says. Especially for Miss Rachel. They were the last of their family."

Trixie was silent for a moment. Then she said soberly, "No wonder she hates that swamp! But I wonder why she still lives there. The fire was forty years ago."

"Dad says that the talk around the bank is that she blames herself for the little girl's death, and living there is a sort of way of punishing herself. Besides, she has no other place to go."

"Why does she blame herself?" Mart asked. "Did she start the fire or something like that?"

Brian shook his head. "No. Dad says it's supposed to have started in the summer kitchen from grease that caught fire on the stove. The house went up so fast that there was hardly time to get some of the priceless antique furniture and family silver out. The servants did what they could, but the flames moved too fast."

"I saw some old trunks up in the barn loft. I suppose they're part of the stuff that was salvaged," Trixie said, "and I saw some lovely old furniture in the cottage when I peeked in this afternoon."

"Miss Snoop," Mart said, and before Trixie could think of something in her own defense, he went on. "I still would like to hear why Miss Rachel thinks she's to blame for what happened to her sister."

"Dad was a little vague about that, but he thought it was because Miss Rachel, as Emily's big sister, had punished her for some mischief and sent her to bed without supper. When the fire started, the servants forgot all about little Emily being up in her bedroom, and it was Rachel herself who found her there, unconscious from the smoke, and brought her down through the smoke and flames. She put the little girl safely on the lawn and then ran back inside again to get some papers of her father's. When she came back, Emily was gone. No one had seen her in all the excitement."

Trixie and Mart had listened intently, shocked by the old tragedy. Mart nodded somberly as his brother ended. "And when they did find her in the swamp it was too late?" he asked.

"That's right," Brian agreed. "And Miss Rachel blamed herself for leaving the child for the few minutes it took her to find her father's papers and save them. She had a nervous breakdown and was in a sanitarium for months. Then she moved into the marsh cottage that had been the servants' quarters, and she's lived there ever since, all alone."

"No wonder she looked as if she'd seen a ghost today," Trixie said with a shudder. "Gaye, with her yellow curls like Emily's, walking out of the barn in what must have been Emily's dress!"

"Who told you what color Emily's hair was?" Brian asked.

"Why, Miss Rachel was talking to me just before Gaye started pounding on the barn door, and she said something about Emily's curls being 'long and yellow, too.'"

The two boys exchanged quick looks. "*Too?*" Mart said quickly. "You mean she *had* already seen Gaye? I thought she denied that."

"Maybe Gaye wasn't lying when she said Miss Rachel had purposely locked her in the barn!" Brian added.

"No, no, *no!* She *hadn't* seen Gaye. *I* told her about Gaye's curls being long and yellow when I went to the door to ask if she had seen Gaye!" Trixie explained.

"That's different," Brian said with relief. "Glad to hear it. I'd hate to think Trent had guessed right about an attempted kidnapping. You had me holding my breath!" He looked suddenly toward the open window, then held up his hand. "Listen!"

They all heard it then. Faintly, from the Wheeler mansion high on the hill beyond the Belden wood lot, the sound of violin music was clear on the night air.

Trixie dashed to the back door and flung it open so they could hear more clearly. "It's Gaye, all right!" she said in an excited whisper. "She got over her sulks!"

At a pause in the music, Brian whispered, "Wow-ee! The kid is good, good, good!"

But Mart snickered. "I bet Miss Crandall would send us a bill if she knew we were enjoying it for free!"

All Trixie said was "Shhh!" as the music started again. She closed her eyes and imagined little Gaye, in the bright gypsy costume of yesterday, standing alone on a stage, her tiny, thin fingers moving expertly on the strings of the big violin while she guided her bow across them, now slowly, now at full tempo, in the flashing gypsy music.

"Nice going," Mart murmured, forgetting to be funny in his real admiration for the little girl's skill.

Trixie frowned and said "Shhh!" again, but just as she said it, the music stopped abruptly in the middle of a particularly brilliant passage.

For a moment they waited in silence, looking at each other inquiringly. But there was no more of the gay gypsy music from the Wheelers'.

"What do you think happened?" Trixie broke the silence after a long moment.

"Mebbe so stling bloke," Mart said in his best pidgin English dialect. "Find more stling; play more!"

Trixie threw a reproachful look at her almost-twin. "It isn't funny. I just hope that's all that's wrong!"

Good Intentions · 13

THERE SHE GOES!" Mart told Brian, with a grin that made Trixie's face redden. "A violin string breaks, and right away she smells a big deal. Har, har!" he teased his sister. "Relax, dearie!"

Brian saw that Trixie's temper was rising. "Relax yourself, son," he told his younger brother. "Trixie's hunches usually pay off. And with that small imp Gaye around, anything could be happening over there at Wheelers' right now. Gaye could have broken the violin over her aunt's head, for instance."

Trixie giggled at the picture his words invoked, and Mart couldn't help joining in.

But there was no more music from the direction of the big Wheeler mansion, and in a very few minutes Trixie and the boys heard the Belden station wagon being driven into the barn-garage.

"Whatever happened up there, it seems to have

broken up the party early," Brian said as he hurried out to greet their parents.

Both of the elder Beldens looked serious as they came in a few seconds later.

"The poor little thing should never have been asked to play tonight, after all she went through today," Moms was saying as she slipped off her coat and scarf.

"Moms! What happened?" Trixie couldn't wait.

"Gaye fainted, poor lamb. She fainted right in the middle of a piece—one of those awfully hard ones. One minute she was playing away, and the next she just crumpled up and fell in a heap on the floor. It was terribly sad. And that Miss Crandall—" She paused and made an angry gesture.

"Well. . . ." Mr. Belden's voice sounded gently but unmistakably reproachful.

"I don't care! That woman is a monster!" Moms was defiant. "She accused that poor little darling of just pretending and tried to drag her to her feet. She actually shook her! But the child just went limp and had to be carried to bed. The doctor said it's a plain, simple case of complete exhaustion, and he's forbidden Gaye to even touch her violin for a week!"

"What's going to be done about next Saturday night's recital?" Mart asked curiously.

"Why, the doctor thinks that if she rests and leads a quiet life, like a normal little girl, for the next week or ten days, she should be able to appear the Saturday after that." Mr. Belden shook his head. "Miss Crandall isn't very happy about postponing it. It upsets their schedule for the rest of the tour. But there's nothing she can do about it, as long as Gaye isn't feeling strong enough to appear."

"The poor little thing is just skin and bones," Moms said indignantly. "It seemed to me yesterday that Miss Crandall wasn't a bit sympathetic with her."

Trixie had her own idea about who deserved the sympathy, but she swallowed hard and held it back. She knew Moms wouldn't like her to feel that way, after promising to do her best to like Gaye.

A few minutes later, she slipped away to the study to phone Honey.

"Do you think she really fainted?" Trixie asked skeptically. "Maybe she was just being temperamental."

"Oh, no!" Honey sounded very sure. "The poor little thing really collapsed. Her face was as white as chalk."

"Dad says she'll be staying on at your house another week, at least," Trixie said. "I suppose she'll be in bed most of the time, and you won't have to entertain her."

"I hope so!" Honey said hastily and then amended it just as quickly. "Oh, I shouldn't have said that. I don't really mean it. I was just being selfish."

"But she *will* be a little pest, I bet," Trixie insisted sulkily. "She'll have to go wherever you go, and it's going to be awfully boring for you."

"I know," Honey admitted. "Only it won't last very long. Miss Crandall says Gaye simply can't 'lay off,' as they call it in their business, because she's booked solid across the country until July."

"That's a funny expression—'booked solid.' What does it mean?" Trixie asked, puzzled. She never minded letting Honey know when she didn't recognize a word or an expression. Honey never teased her about being ignorant the way Mart usually did.

"It means she'll appear somewhere for a concert on one night and then have to travel to another city the next day to do the whole thing over again."

Trixie said a small "Oh" and thought it over for a second. Then she said impulsively, "I'm glad I'm just plain me and not a famous somebody-or-other! Imagine all that traveling around! And being bullied by Miss Crandall! But I suppose Gaye gets a nice long vacation after the end of the tour."

"Oh, no," Honey said quickly. "Miss Trask says Gaye has to keep learning new concertos and stuff all the time, for the next season."

"I feel kind of sorry for her," Trixie admitted, "even though I know she's a little monster."

"I do, too, really," Honey agreed. "I've decided that I'll try to be extra nice to her while she's here."

Trixie sighed. "I suppose we all should. Moms says so, anyhow, and she's usually right."

So they agreed most solemnly to overlook any small impudence on Gaye's part and try to make her stay at Sleepyside a happy one.

Trixie was just saying good-bye, when she heard a small sound at the doorway. She was so sure it was Mart that she said, without turning around, "I fooled you, Smarty Marty. I'm all through talking, so there's no use in your sneaking around listening!" She hung up the receiver and whirled to face the door, a saucy grin on her face.

But it wasn't her almost-twin who was standing there.

It was a small figure in pajamas. "I waited an' waited," it reproached her accusingly, "but you didn't come. What did Gaye say? Can she go with us?"

"I wasn't talking to Gaye, Bobby. That was Honey. Gaye's sort of sick, and I don't think she'll feel very much like going out picking flowers tomorrow. We'll have to put it off till some other day."

"But I don't want to! You said we'd go tomorrow after Sunday school and take Gaye! You're mean!" Bobby burst into sobs. "You don't like Gaye!"

Trixie hurried to him and put her arms around him. "Now, Bobby," she said gently, "you mustn't say that. Gaye *is* sick or I wouldn't tell you so. And after Sunday school, we'll come home so I can change into my jeans and a sweater and you can put on your playclothes. Then we'll take Gaye some of those pretty flowers that Honey and I picked yesterday. You can give them to her all by your own little self—if Miss Crandall will let you see her."

Bobby's tears disappeared in a flash, and he gave Trixie a big hug. "I love you lots," he confided.

And a few minutes later, after he had meekly allowed her to lead him upstairs and tumble him back into bed, he told her sleepily, "I'm gonna tell Gaye 'bout my new chickies. Do you think she'd like a yellow one?"

"You can ask her tomorrow, lambkin," Trixie told him cheerfully, but to herself she added silently, *if she bothers to see you.*

Honey was saddling Starlight inside the Wheeler stable as Trixie and Bobby came trudging up the long driveway after Sunday school the next morning.

Their shadows stretched out across the stable floor as they stood in the doorway, and Honey turned quickly.

The first thing that Trixie noticed was that Honey's pretty face was unusually sober.

"Hey, where are the boys and Regan? And didn't Mart come over to ride Starlight? What's going on?" Trixie asked it all in one breath.

"Oh, hi!" Honey answered, summoning up a smile, but with a warning nod in Bobby's direction as he stood in the square of sunlight in the doorway, clutching the wild flowers by their tissue-wrapped stems. "Hi, Bobby! Did you bring me the pretty flowers?"

Bobby shook his head. "No!" He put the flowers hastily behind him. "Flowers for Gaye! Where's Gaye?"

"Gulp!" Honey's eyes twinkled. "I guess that puts me very nicely in my place." The twinkle faded quickly.

"Anything wrong?" Trixie asked under her breath as she took a couple of quick steps toward Honey.

"Tell you in a minute," Honey said in a whisper. "Bobby!" She raised her voice as Bobby came in farther, looking around. "Gaye's up at the house. She's probably having breakfast right now, and I think if you asked Miss Crandall very nicely, she'd let you take the flowers in to Gaye. Do you want to?"

"Oh, yes!" Bobby, with a beaming smile, was out and away like a flash.

"Such devotion!" Honey laughed. Then she nodded toward Strawberry's stall, where the mare was moving restlessly. "None of them has had a workout this morning. Why don't you saddle up Strawberry? Let's take her and Starlight for a good run."

"Swell! Do you think it's all right to leave Bobby? I didn't figure on riding this morning."

"He'll be all right. When your mother phoned Miss Trask a few minutes ago to say you were both on your way over, I asked Miss Trask to watch out for him while you and I gave the horses a run."

"Oh, grand! Honey, you're positively a brain. You always think of everything!" Trixie dashed over to the tack room and brought out a saddle and the rest of her riding gear. Then she got Strawberry out of her stall and brought her over close to Starlight. She started to saddle Strawberry. "Okay. Now tell me what's going on."

"Well, in the first place, there's nothing exciting to tell about Regan or the boys. They're all over at Mr. Maypenny's. His ground dried out faster than he expected, so he decided he'd better plant that corn today instead of tomorrow. They're all lending a hand. So you and I are stuck with exercising these two beasts."

"That's not hard to take," Trixie chuckled. "But why did you want Bobby to go away while you told me? He wouldn't have wanted to go along with us—not while little Miss Gaye is here!"

"It's Paul Trent. He came over to see Miss Crandall a while ago and told her that he still thought *somebody* had put Gaye up to hiding and pretending she had been kidnapped."

"How silly can he get?" Trixie said scornfully. "I hope that she showed him the door!"

"Not right away. She believed him at first and called Dad in to listen. Dad really told *Mr.* Trent what he thought of him! The big troublemaker ducked out with his tail between his legs, as Mart would say!"

"I should think he'd be ashamed of himself, trying to start trouble that way. I hope he's cured now." Trixie had her doubts, but she didn't want to say so to Honey.

"I'm sure he is!" Honey said confidently. Then she glanced at her wristwatch and looked startled. "Goodness! We'd better get started. Which way should we ride today?"

Trixie thought hard for a moment. Then she grinned. "Why don't we ride out to Miss Rachel's and let her offer us that hot mint tea she mentioned yesterday? If we like it, we can get the recipe for Miss Bennett. It would be nice if we could add that recipe to our bunches of swamp plants."

"That's a wonderful idea!" Honey agreed as she swung into Starlight's saddle. "And away we go!"

They rode along Glen Road at a trot and were soon at the turnoff that led to Martin's Marsh.

"Things look a lot different when the sun is shining, don't they?" Trixie called to Honey as they turned in and started up the narrow road. "But it's still awfully squishy. I'm getting muddy."

"Me, too." Honey brushed a spot of mud off her saddle. "We'll have some cleaning up to do to pass Regan's inspection when we get home!"

They were passing the burnt-out mansion when Trixie slowed down. "Golly, Honey! It looks gloomy and mysterious even in the sunshine. Sad, too, now that we know about poor little Emily and Miss Rachel."

"It must have been the biggest house in the valley," Honey said, shaking her head. "They must have been

awfully rich to be able to keep up a place like that.
Goodness knows, ours is only half that size, and Dad
says it's a white elephant." She giggled. "That was probably a whole herd of white elephants."

They rode on and soon came in sight of the small
white cottage. But they reined in as they stared at the
car parked in front of the gate. Someone was calling on
Miss Rachel Martin.

"Well, I guess we might as well turn around and go
home. It's probably somebody who'll stay all afternoon
drinking *our* mint tea," Trixie moaned. "And I was
hoping I could dazzle Miss Bennett with the recipe
tomorrow morning! She's collecting all sorts of herb
recipes for her book."

"Book?" Honey queried as they turned back toward
the main road. "Is that why she's so keen on herbs and
swamp plants?"

"Oh, yes. Miss Bennett says that when the pioneers
were living in deep forests miles and miles from any
doctors, they had to make up remedies for practically
everything. I suppose they had to experiment a lot before they found the right ones. Of course, they learned
a lot from the Indians."

Honey looked impressed. "I never thought of the
Indians as people who needed medicine. The pictures
always show them marvelously healthy, even if they
must have nearly frozen lots of times, not wearing much
clothing!"

"Oh, Miss Bennett says they had remedies for all sorts
of illnesses and accidents. You'd never believe some of
the things they used ordinary little weeds for. Like the

one they called boneset. The Indians believed it would make broken bones heal fast, and when the white men tried it, it worked just fine."

"How did they use it?" Honey's eyes opened wide.

"They made a poultice of the dried leaves and tied it on the arm or leg or whatever bone was broken, and the bone knit fast. Miss Bennett says part of the treatment was that the broken bone had to be kept perfectly still for a certain length of time, and perhaps *that* was why it healed so quickly, and not the boneset poultice. But she says the plant does have a lot of calcium in it, so maybe it did help."

"Anyhow, they thought it did. That's what counts."

"I was hoping we could talk to Miss Rachel about boneset and some of the other things we gathered in the swamp." Trixie frowned.

"Oh, well, you can tell Miss Bennett about the mint tea we didn't get, and I'm sure if you promise to get her the recipe *next* Saturday or Sunday, you'll get the good marks for the project, anyway!" Honey laughed as she and Trixie guided their horses down onto the wider road and stepped up their pace.

They had gone only a few yards when a car came roaring down out of the narrow road and passed them, within a foot of Trixie's mare. The mare reared, and it took all of Trixie's horsemanship to stay in the saddle.

By the time the mare was calm again, the car was out of sight, but they had both recognized it. It was the car they had seen parked outside of Miss Rachel's cottage.

And the driver was Paul Trent.

Trouble Brewing • 14

WHAT DO YOU SUPPOSE he was doing up at Miss Rachel's place?" Trixie asked with a frown.

"Probably trying to get her to confess she was in on the kidnapping fake," Honey replied scornfully.

"Well, from the look on his face, she told him off, loud and clear," Trixie said. "He was certainly upset about something." She had a sudden inspiration. "Maybe we should go back and let her tell us about it."

"Huh-uh." Honey shook her head firmly. "Let's wait till after school tomorrow. Maybe Di can come along. She's sure to love that little old cottage and the garden."

So they rode homeward, chatting easily and making plans to bring Miss Rachel a basketful of Mrs. Belden's home-canned fruit as a gift.

But when they reached the foot of the Wheelers' driveway and paused, as usual, to gaze with pride at their little clubhouse, they were surprised to see the door wide open. They could hear the sound of voices.

"That's Jim laughing," Honey said, surprised. "I thought he and your brothers were going to be planting all day for Mr. Maypenny. They must have finished early."

"I hear Mart's voice, too," Trixie said with a little frown. "Wonder what they're laughing about."

Another outburst of laughter made them exchange quick looks. They both had recognized Bobby's shrill giggles coming from the clubhouse.

"There's something going on, and I'm not going to miss it," Trixie declared. "Let's take a quick look before we put these critters of ours to bed."

They dismounted hastily and tied the mares to the fence post. An outburst of handclaps startled them both.

"I'm sure I heard Gaye laughing just then," Honey said as they hurried up the brick walk.

"Gaye? After collapsing last night and all?" Trixie asked, surprised. They both hurried faster to see.

As they reached the door, they heard Jim's voice. "Say, that's a keen trick, Gaye. Where did he ever learn to dance like that?"

"I taught him myself, of course," came Gaye's reply. "He wouldn't learn from anyone but me."

As the girls looked into the clubroom, they were astonished to see Mr. Poo waltzing around on his hind legs and balancing a small, brightly painted stick across his aristocratic nose as he danced. Gaye, sitting cross-legged on the table, was guiding him with motions of her hand, while Jim, Mart, Brian, and Bobby watched with approval.

"He can do lots more tricks," Gaye said in a bored

voice, "but that's enough for now." She stopped waving her hand, and the poodle dropped to all fours, picked up the fallen baton with his teeth, and went to lie down with it across his paws. He kept bright eyes on his little mistress, alert for another signal to perform.

"He's a whiz, all right. And so are you, kid!" Mart told Gaye seriously.

Jim saw the girls in the doorway. "Hey, Madame President, Honey, both of you come on in and take a look at what Mr. Poo's learned to do!"

"Yeah, maybe you can teach that Reddy of yours some of these tricks!" Mart added with a laugh as Trixie hesitated.

She reddened and then sniffed disdainfully at them. "Don't be silly," she said. "Reddy couldn't be bothered learning a lot of silly show-off stuff like that. He's a *real* dog!"

"Oh!" Gaye glared at Trixie and slid down off the table. "I hate you! You're mean and horrid! Come, Mr. Poo!" She ran to the door and out before any of them realized she was going. The little dog frisked after her.

They could hear her crying as she ran down the path to the driveway. Everyone stared disapprovingly at the startled Trixie, and Bobby burst into tears.

"Oh, Trix! You've hurt the poor child's feelings!" Honey said reproachfully. "You know she adores that puppy!"

Mart snorted at Trixie. "Just because you can't waltz with a stick on your nose, you get jealous of a poodle!"

"Oh, I didn't mean to hurt her feelings," Trixie stammered. "I was just standing up for Reddy!" She looked appealingly at Brian, but he shook his head and looked grim. It was too much for her. Brian was always her champion. She turned and ran out.

There was a moment of silence. Then Honey said weakly, "After all, Mart, you didn't have to be that sarcastic. Trix didn't mean to—" She broke off abruptly as she was interrupted by Trixie's call.

"Jim, Brian! Hurry! Gaye's fallen and hurt herself!" There was fear in the voice, and they all heard it. Jim was the first to reach the door, but the others were close on his heels, with Honey bringing up the rear and holding Bobby's hand.

They saw Gaye lying in a crumpled heap in the middle of the driveway. The small poodle was standing guard beside her motionless figure. When he saw them coming, he started to bark defiantly.

Trixie reached Gaye's side first and knelt down by her. "It's all right, Mr. Poo," she told the poodle. "We're going to help her." He whimpered and lay down beside Gaye, watching alertly as Jim and Brian came up quickly and knelt down opposite Trixie.

Brian motioned them all to stand back as he made a cautious examination. Bobby was crying loudly, and Honey was having difficulty holding him back from rushing to Gaye. "Somebody hurted Gaye!" he wailed, struggling with Honey.

Brian looked up at him. "It's all right, Bobby. Hush, now. She just tripped and knocked herself out. She'll be okay in a minute."

Bobby stopped struggling. If Brian said Gaye was all right, that was good enough for Bobby. He had faith in Brian because Brian never teased him as Mart did.

"We'd better carry her up to the house," suggested Jim.

"She's coming out of it now," Brian told him. "She's got a small bump on her forehead, but that's about all."

Gaye's eyelids fluttered, and she looked up at them with a sad little moan.

Trixie asked anxiously, "Oh, Gaye! Do you feel all right now?"

Gaye frowned at her and struggled to sit up. Jim and Brian helped her, and Jim kept his arm around her shoulders to support her. "Just sit still a couple of minutes, and you'll feel okay," Brian told her, but she shoved him aside and glared at Trixie.

"Go away! I don't like you!" she told Trixie.

Trixie flushed, but she stayed where she was. "I'm sorry I made you angry. Mr. Poo is a fine little dog, and he's awfully brave. Just as brave as Reddy."

Gaye looked surprised. She studied Trixie a moment and then demanded with a frown, "How do *you* know?" She leaned over, put her arm around the poodle, and drew him close to her as she stared into Trixie's face.

"Why, the other day in our orchard, when he ran after Reddy, I saw Mr. Poo actually try to attack a snake, all by himself, till I called him off! It was the bravest thing!" Trixie said earnestly.

"Really?" Gaye's eyes sparkled, and she smiled at Trixie with real warmth for the first time. "An honest-to-goodness real snake?"

"I should say it was! A poisonous one!" Trixie answered her gravely. "But Mr. Poo wasn't the least bit scared of it, though it coiled and hissed at him."

"Oh-h!" Gaye shuddered. Then she gave the poodle a hug and laid her cheek tenderly against his fluffy top-knot. "He *is* awfully brave. He's not afraid of anything. He's my best friend, and we love each other." The poodle licked the tip of her nose, as if he agreed, and then barked happily.

They helped Gaye to her feet. Though she seemed a little unsteady for a moment, she got over it at once, and she and Bobby were soon running hand in hand up the driveway.

"That story about Mr. Poodle Poo attacking the snake is pure fiction, and we know it!" Mart grinned as he shook a warning finger at Trixie.

"Well, he was walking straight toward it when I called him back. He *could* have been going to attack it," Trixie admitted with a giggle. "Anyhow, I made her feel a little friendlier. I actually got a smile from her!"

"So, Mart, my lad"—Brian waved his hand—"Trixie didn't really fib. It was like your telling Di that you did all right in that math exam last week, when actually you only passed by the skin of your teeth!"

Mart flushed as the girls giggled and Jim fought back a smile. They all knew that he was anxious to have Di admire him. It was obvious that he couldn't think of anything to say for a moment, but when his eyes fell on the horses tied to the fence post, he scowled at Trixie and nodded toward them. "I'd hate to be in your shoes, Miss Trixie Belden, if Regan sees where you left Straw-berry, standing in the wind!"

"Gleeps! Thanks for reminding me, Mart," Trixie said hastily. "Come on, Honey. We'll do our duty, even though we're fainting from fatigue!" She gave the boys a hopeful look.

"Not a chance," Brian said promptly. "You roped us into doing your work for you yesterday. Today you do it yourself!" Jim agreed, with a vigorous nod and a twinkle in his eye at Trixie's disappointed pout.

"Okay," she said with a heavy sigh of resignation. "But if I should faint from exhaustion, you'll have to finish."

"Oh-oh! Don't be a copycat, sister dear!" Brian chuckled. "It's a good act only when Gaye does it!"

"You mean she didn't really knock herself unconscious just now? She was only making believe?" Trixie asked, her cheeks beginning to burn and her blue eyes flashing.

Brian grinned and pretended to stroke an imaginary beard. "Doctors never tell," he said in as deep a voice as he could manage.

"I wondered about that." Honey giggled. "She could not have fallen hard enough. I think she *was* a little stunned, and when she heard Trixie calling us, she just couldn't resist acting a little."

"She certainly fooled me!" Trixie said angrily.

"I wouldn't let it upset me, if I were you," Jim said gently. "You're a friend of Gaye's now, because you said kind things about the puppy. And from what I've seen of the poor kid, she needs friends."

"I suppose so," Trixie admitted. Then she smiled. "At least I know now that prodigies have *some* feelings."

"She adores that little dog," Honey commented as she and Trixie were grooming their horses a few minutes later. "Look at her and Bobby romping up there with him now."

Trixie looked up toward the wide expanse of lawn. Gaye was chasing Bobby across the lawn, with Mr. Poo running at their heels. They were laughing and shouting. "Bobby's having the time of his life," Trixie said a little wistfully and went back to her job.

Honey looked at her mischievously. "There's green in those blue eyes, Miss Belden!" She laughed, but the laugh stopped as she looked up toward the romping youngsters again. "Oh, dear, wouldn't you know it?" she said disgustedly. "Here comes trouble!"

Trixie looked and nodded agreement. Miss Crandall had suddenly emerged from the house and was stalking after Gaye. They watched her corner Gaye and then take her firmly by the arm and lead her into the house. The little dog romped after them, and the door was closed in Bobby's face. He stood looking at the closed door for a long moment and then turned with an aimless air and wandered over toward the garage, where the boys were talking to Regan.

"The course of true love," Honey said lightly, "has hit a detour."

But Trixie, although she smiled a little at Honey's joking remark, looked serious a moment afterward. "I guess," she told Honey, "when a person is a prodigy, it's wrong to have fun and want to play like ordinary people. I'm glad I'm not gifted. It must be sort of like being in a prison."

"I suppose that's how it seems to Gaye, but maybe Miss Crandall is really worried about Gaye's health and thinks she's better off resting than running around, getting even more tired than she's been." Honey tried to see the other side of it, though her sympathy was with Gaye.

A little later, as Trixie helped her mother prepare the late Sunday afternoon dinner, she found that Moms agreed with Honey.

"Gaye must be quite a handful for her aunt," Mrs. Belden told Trixie. "I hope she won't get any more ideas of hiding from Miss Crandall the way she did yesterday. I'm glad that was all straightened out, so there won't be any silly stories in the paper about 'kidnapping' her."

"I'm glad, too," Trixie admitted. "I was worried over what that reporter said to us about a stunt to sell tickets. He almost said I had thought it up and the Bob-Whites were mixed up in it."

"People say things when they're angry—or humiliated, as he apparently was by Sergeant Rooney's teasing him," Moms explained gently. "I'm sure he didn't mean half of it."

"He sounded as if he did," Trixie said stubbornly, "and this morning he tried to make a big thing out of it to Miss Crandall, and she almost believed him."

"I'm sure Honey's father settled all that for good," Moms assured her. "Stop thinking about it. It's all over."

Trixie was almost able to believe that—until she came down to breakfast the next morning.

The Twisted Story • 15

MORNING, EVERYBODY," Trixie said cheerfully, bouncing into the kitchen and dropping her books and sweater on the chair by the door so she could grab them and run for the bus when it was due.

Her father and mother and the boys were all at the table, eating quietly. Only Moms managed a subdued "Good morning, dear."

Trixie looked around at them. "What's wrong?"

Mart nodded glumly toward her place. "Look at your little surprise. Second column, front page."

It was only then that she noticed the morning newspaper lying across her plate. She dashed to pick it up and look where Mart had told her to.

The heading was GAYE GOES FOR A RIDE. Trixie gasped and looked weakly around the table. Bobby was the only one who wasn't watching her. He was busy eating.

Mr. Belden said sternly, "I don't know what you said or did to antagonize the young man who wrote that

151

column, but it seems to have had a bad effect."

Trixie sank into her chair and bent her head over the paper. She read silently for a couple of minutes, then read the last paragraph of the article over again out loud, hardly believing it.

" 'Miss Trixie Belden of Sleepyside Junior-Senior High School took a prominent part in the finding of the missing child. Miss Belden, age thirteen, has acquired quite a reputation for solving mysteries. It is even rumored that the Bob-Whites of the Glen, an exclusive group at the school, are thinking of changing their name to The Belden Private Eyes and specializing in publicity stunts for a selected list of clients. Miss Trixie "Sherlock Holmes" Belden is their president, as it happens.'

"Oh!" Trixie's eyes flashed. "That's not fair! He makes it sound as if the Bob-Whites, and especially Trixie Belden, had arranged the whole thing for publicity!"

"It could be taken that way," her father said grimly.

"Can't we make him take it back? Can't you talk to the editor of the *Sun?*" Trixie demanded.

Mr. Belden shook his head. "I'm afraid not. He's been clever enough not to make a direct charge that any of you arranged Gaye's disappearance. He hinted at it, of course. But he didn't actually say so. The best thing you and the Bob-Whites can do is to ignore that part of the story." He frowned. "I'd advise you to avoid any comment on it to him. Just ignore it."

"Dad's right, dear," Moms assured Trixie, who was frowning rebelliously. "After all, it's probably only his idea of teasing you."

Mart growled, "I'd like to take a poke at him!"

"You'll do nothing of the kind!" his father said.

There was general silence for a moment as the three Bob-Whites exchanged resigned looks and then went on eating their breakfast.

Moms sighed as she saw their long faces. She looked appealingly at their father. "You could say something to the editor about the rest of the article, though, couldn't you? I mean where he says that Miss Martin thought she was seeing a ghost when Gaye came out of the barn dressed in the other little girl's clothes. He makes it sound as if Miss Martin weren't quite sane!"

"And Miss Martin was just surprised when she saw Gaye in a dress she recognized as Emily's, that's all," Trixie said. "She knew it wasn't little Emily's ghost!"

"I don't think anyone will take his word for it, especially anyone who has ever talked to Miss Rachel," her father said lightly. "She was an excellent business-woman until the highway took away the passing cars and left her high and dry out there."

"What did she sell?" Trixie asked, surprised.

"Marvelous hooked rugs that she made herself," her mother said quickly, "and old-fashioned patchwork quilts that people came from all over the valley to buy. You children each have one of her double-wedding-ring quilts on your bed."

"But if she doesn't sell anything anymore, how can she live, all alone out there? Doesn't it cost money?" Trixie was always practical.

"You wondered the same thing about Mr. Maypenny, your 'poacher,' who turned out to own a nice piece of land in the middle of the Wheelers' game preserve. He raised most of the food he needed. He trapped otter and mink in the streams and sold their skins for sugar, salt, and coffee—things that he couldn't grow. Miss Rachel gets along without those things now, I imagine, just as our pioneer ancestors did," Mr. Belden explained.

"Yikes!" Brian said, looking at his wristwatch. "Bobby's bus is just about due, Trix. Better move!"

For the time being, there was no more talk about either the brash young reporter or Miss Rachel Martin.

But that afternoon, as Honey, Di, and Trixie got off the bus at the Wheeler stop, one of their schoolmates called out through the open window jokingly, "G'bye, Miss Sherlock Holmes Belden!" There were noisy giggles from several others as the bus pulled away.

"Don't pay any attention to those dopes," pretty, violet-eyed Diana Lynch told Trixie, glaring after the bus. "They'll forget that silly article by tomorrow."

"Golly, I hope so," Trixie said unhappily. "That's all I've been hearing all day—that and people making believe they're ghosts and going 'whoo-whoo' at me!"

When they reached the stable, the prospect of taking a ride in the bright spring sunshine wiped out Trixie's annoyance. Regan had saddled Lady, Strawberry, and Starlight, and the horses were standing waiting.

Mrs. Belden had sent a basket of preserves and jellies over earlier with Mr. Belden, who had dropped it off on his way to work at the bank.

"Don't ride off and forget the present," Regan reminded them. "I guess the old lady'll be glad to get it. Give her a change of diet. 'Specially the crab apple."

Honey reminded the girls, "Let's hurry and change

to riding things, so we can get started. I'm dying to get better acquainted with Miss Rachel."

"I want to meet her, too," Diana seconded as they started up toward the house to change.

After just a few steps, they were surprised to see Tom Delanoy, the chauffeur, backing Mrs. Wheeler's big car away from the house, turning it on the driveway, and coming down toward them. From a distance, the car looked empty, except for Tom.

The girls stepped aside, but to their amazement he stopped the car beside them.

"Hi!" He grinned. "Your mom says you're to go along to Miss Martin's with us, Honey."

"Us?" Honey asked. She stepped to the car and looked inside. Gaye was huddled in the rear, as far in the corner as she could get. She had Mr. Poo tight in her arms as she stared unsmilingly at Honey. The delicate white dress was very carefully arranged on the driver's seat next to Tom.

"But we were going to ride out that way, all three of us. Can't we take the dress in a package on one of our saddles?" Honey frowned.

"Well, your mother said—" Tom looked uneasy.

Gaye leaned forward, scowling. "You don't need to come with me! I'm not afraid of that mean old witch!" she said defiantly but with a telltale quaver.

It was Trixie who noticed that little quaver in Gaye's voice. She said quickly, "Maybe we can all three go in style! Let the boys exercise the horses this afternoon. We can take their turns tomorrow afternoon, as a swap. How about it, Honey?"

"Why not? They're always asking us to take *their* turns for some excuse or other!" Honey agreed happily.

"I'll break the news to them," Regan said promptly. "But you'd better climb in and get started, before they arrive and begin making excuses about why they can't do it!" He handed the basket of preserves to Trixie. "And don't forget the present."

They hurriedly swarmed into the big car, and almost at once they were on their way. Gaye had been strangely silent since her one outburst. The girls began to feel uncomfortable as she stared out the car window.

"What an adorable dog!" Di said, after a long silence. "May I pet him?"

Gaye bit her lower lip. Then she nodded.

Di stroked the fluffy white head and told Gaye what a darling he was. But Gaye looked accusingly at Trixie. "I guess you didn't mean it when you said you liked Mr. Poo," she said in a small, hurt voice. "You didn't even say hello to him."

Trixie smiled. "I wanted to, but I wasn't sure if *he* liked *me*. Those teeth look pretty sharp."

Gaye giggled and hugged her pet. Then she bent down and pretended to listen to something he was saying. When she lifted her head, she was smiling. "He says he wouldn't think of biting you, because he wants you to be his friend."

Trixie patted the little dog's back. "I'd love to, Mr. Poo," she told him seriously, "and I'd like to be Gaye's friend, too."

Gaye stared at her doubtfully, and they could all see that she wasn't sure just what to say. Honey spoke promptly. "We'd all like to be your friends, Gaye. We think you're just wonderful. I never heard anyone play the violin as beautifully as you do."

"It must be super to be so gifted," Di sighed.

But instead of seeming to enjoy the compliments, Gaye frowned and leaned back to stare out of the window steadily. A shadow seemed to come over her face.

The girls exchanged puzzled looks. It seemed to all of them a strange way of acting when they had sincerely tried to compliment her.

Di tried again. "Is it really true that you've played before kings and queens, Gaye?" she asked with awe.

Gaye scowled and didn't answer for a moment. Then she shrugged impatiently. "Oh, I guess so," she said indifferently. "Aunt Della said they were. But they're all just audiences. I play the same pieces for them as I do for the others. We stay in hotels and always keep traveling. Places are all the same, and so are audiences." She gave a weary little sigh and slumped in her corner.

Trixie felt a tug of sympathy, but she couldn't think of anything to say. She was glad when Tom turned his head to warn them, with a grin, "Hold on, ladies! We're about to go over the bumps!" And a moment later, they were all giggling and bouncing around in the car as it negotiated the narrow, rough road to Miss Rachel's cottage.

Miss Rachel was working in her flower garden as they drove up. She rose with a frown as the car stopped. But the frown disappeared when she recognized Trixie getting out. And she was most gracious as she invited the girls and the chauffeur to have a cup of mint tea.

Tom refused hastily but politely. "I'll just stay out here and wait for them, Miss Rachel. Only, don't let them stay long and bother you."

"I'm sure they'll be no bother," she assured him. "Come along, children."

Honey, Trixie, and Di started in with her, but Gaye held back, the poodle in her arms. "I think I'll stay here," she said wistfully. "Mr. Poo doesn't like me to leave him."

"But he's very welcome, too, child," Miss Rachel assured her. "We may even be able to find him a cookie."

They all trooped into the cottage, Trixie carrying the gift of preserves and Gaye holding the starched white dress. Miss Rachel gazed at the dress admiringly.

"It's done up beautifully, dear," she told Gaye. "I'll hang it carefully away, in case some other young lady wants to borrow it someday."

"It's a very pretty dress, and I thank you," Gaye said gravely, "and I'm sorry I was so upset yesterday."

"That's all right, child. Just forget it, and let's go put the kettle on for that good hot mint tea."

As Gaye and the poodle went cheerfully to the kitchen with Miss Rachel, the three Bob-Whites exchanged pleased looks.

"She isn't really such a little monster when you dig down, is she?" Honey asked Trixie, and Trixie had to admit that Honey was right.

Aftereffects · 16

WE ALMOST CAME to see you yesterday," Trixie told Miss Rachel between sips of the hot herb tea. The small cottage living room was bright with sunlight as they sat with Honey and Di and little Gaye and chatted politely.

"I wish you had, child." Miss Rachel smiled. "Why didn't you?"

"Well—" Trixie paused and looked to Honey for assistance—"you see, we met Paul Trent when he left here in a hurry, and he looked so mean and angry that we were afraid he had upset you about something."

"And so we just didn't want to intrude on you," Honey added.

Miss Rachel frowned and rocked silently in the low rocking chair that looked as if it had been made in Colonial days. "Mr. Trent is a thoughtless young man. He came here asking me some very personal questions about my family history, and when I hesitated to answer them, he made insulting remarks about my ancestors, and I ordered him to leave."

"I should think you would!" Trixie said fiercely. "He's just plain disagreeable." Her own resentment was still simmering.

"Well, I think we'll just forget that young man now and enjoy our visit," Miss Rachel said. "I believe there are more cupcakes in my pantry." She went out to see if she could find them.

"Do you think we should tell her about the story in this morning's *Sun?*" Trixie whispered hastily to Honey and Di.

"Oh, no! There's no use upsetting her again," Honey answered softly, and Di nodded her agreement.

When Miss Rachel came back, in triumph, with a newly filled cake plate, they talked about her herb collection and the recipe for the delicious mint tea.

"I'm very proud of my herb garden," Miss Martin told them as she led the way outside to the neat little plot. "There's my Oswego tea. Some call it bee balm. Our pioneer families used it for reducing fever. That's wood sorrel over there. I transplanted it from the marsh. It's very tasty in a salad when it's young." She told them the names of so many that they gave up trying to remember them, and they made her promise that she'd make a list of them soon, so they could come out again to get it, along with some samples of herbs for the botany class.

"And please don't forget the recipe for this tea," Di reminded her.

"You shall have that now," Miss Rachel promised and went to the small rosewood desk in the corner to get pencil and paper.

"Oh, what a lovely brass box!" Trixie exclaimed. She hadn't noticed it on top of the desk before. It was about a foot wide and six inches deep, and it was deeply embossed on all sides with the writhing forms of dragons. On top, a large, ferocious-looking dragon, with five claws on each foot, was devouring a smaller one.

"My great-grandfather brought it from China on one of his voyages," Miss Rachel told them, pleased, as she lifted the heavy box and handed it to Trixie to examine.

"Look at those green eyes!" Trixie said admiringly and touched the big dragon's inlaid eyes. "He's gorgeous."

"He should be!" Miss Rachel laughed. "He's an imperial dragon. Only imperial dragons have five claws."

The girls studied the battle admiringly. Trixie giggled. "Looks like old five-claw is winning."

"Imperial dragons always won, or the imperial ruler would have cut off the artist's head in those days," Miss Rachel said with a little laugh. "It's a very old box."

"I like the green eyes." Trixie rubbed her fingers over the stones that seemed to send out green rays in the sunlight. "I guess he's the original green-eyed monster people keep talking about."

"You should recognize him if he is!" Honey teased, with a meaningful look toward Gaye, who was quite absorbed in trying to finish the last of the cupcakes and keep Mr. Poo from getting more than she did.

Trixie wrinkled her nose at her friend and then put the box down reluctantly. "Good-bye, beautiful," she told the dragon, with a final pat on his menacing brow. "You go ahead and enjoy your fun."

"Goodness, it *is* time to leave!" Di agreed.

In a few minutes they were on their way home in the car.

"She's a darling," Honey said, glancing back toward the cottage as they turned the bend in the road. "I wonder what Trent said about her family that was insulting."

"Oh, probably that old silly about being in partnership with the pirate." Trixie shrugged. "You remember—about the pirate gold being hidden in Martin's Marsh."

Gaye had been huddled, half-asleep, with Mr. Poo cuddled in her arms. She sat up suddenly, staring at Trixie. "Pirate gold? In the swamp?"

Trixie waved it aside and laughed. "There never was any there, of course. But a lot of people believed it."

"Wasn't any *ever* found there?" Gaye persisted.

"Of course not! People found snakes and quicksand and all sorts of accidents but never any sign of gold," Honey assured her. "It's a gruesome place. Br-r-r!"

"I wouldn't be afraid to look," Gaye said thoughtfully, stroking Mr. Poo's head. "I'd take Mr. Poo along, and we'd have no trouble finding it, I'm sure."

Tom Delanoy turned and grinned back at them. "Better not let your Aunt Della hear you, Miss Gaye. She might think you meant that."

"I do!" Gaye said defiantly. "Mr. Poo would chew up the snakes, and I'd dig up the gold, and I'd give it to Aunt Della, and then I wouldn't ever have to play my old violin again or go traveling all the time when I'm tired!" There was a break in her voice as she finished.

Honey and the shocked Di exchanged looks of dismay, but Trixie motioned them not to say anything. Gaye bent her head over and rested it on Mr. Poo's soft coat. Trixie couldn't see her face, but she felt quite sure that the little girl was in tears.

They were glad to be turning just then into the Wheeler driveway. Nobody knew what to say.

Miss Crandall was waiting for Gaye at the garage. She lost no time in ordering her up to the house, and when Gaye, sullen and silent, had reluctantly gone, with the small poodle cavorting after her, her aunt turned to the girls.

"We have decided that Gaye is quite recovered from her nervous attack, and she will be giving her recital a week from Saturday," Miss Crandall said coldly. "So I must ask you to help avoid any more excitement for her. Please don't think I am too severe, Honey. Your mother agrees with me; Gaye's career is too important for her to take any chances with it."

"It wasn't exciting at the marsh, Miss Crandall," Trixie said quickly. "Miss Martin was sweet about the dress. And she likes Gaye. We had a nice visit."

"Nevertheless, she is not to go out there again for any reason," Miss Crandall said with finality and went up to the house after Gaye.

Trixie made a small grimace after her and told Honey, "It looks as if you won't have the little prodigy on your hands to entertain the rest of this week!"

"I'm almost sorry I won't, now that we know her better," Honey said sincerely. "Poor little thing!"

And both Trixie and Di agreed with her.

Mr. Belden came home a couple of hours later as Trixie was telling Mart and Brian about the visit to Miss Martin.

". . . so Miss Rachel practically threw old Trent out for saying mean things about her ancestors. That's why he was so catty in this morning's *Sun* about her 'seeing ghosts,'" she finished. "He's disgusting!"

"I'm inclined to agree," their father said, coming into the room with a grim look on his face.

"Oh," Trixie said weakly. "I bet everybody at the bank was laughing at what he said about me, weren't they?"

"Not at all," her father assured her gravely. "Hardly anyone mentioned it. It's Rachel Martin whom his story has hurt."

"*Hurt?*" Trixie was amazed.

Her father nodded. "You see, that little hint of Trent's that Miss Rachel thought Gaye was her sister's ghost has convinced people that the last of the Martins has failed mentally because of her age and being allowed to live out there alone by the swamp for so long. There's quite a lot of indignation that she's been neglected all this time. The hint about her having her name used as publicity for Gaye has only made it worse."

"But that's just Trent's mean story! Can't we make the *Sun* tell what really happened?" Trixie begged.

"I'm afraid it's a bit late to do anything," her father said gently. "You see, dear, there seems to be something magical about printer's ink. Once people read a story in a newspaper, most of them believe that story is true, even if it's retracted."

"Bud Brown, whose dad is on the city council, told me the council had a special session about it today and decided to take steps to protect Miss Rachel Martin," Brian told them. "I hadn't gotten around yet to telling you about it, Trix, but I meant to."

Trixie looked unhappy. "What do they mean by that?"

"I don't know," Brian admitted and looked inquiringly at his father. But Mr. Belden shook his head.

"It's my fault," Trixie said miserably. "I had to go out hunting for Gaye, and that's what started all this." A big tear started to roll down her cheek. Such weakness was so unusual for her that Mart scowled blackly and exclaimed, "Quit going feminine on us, toots! I'm the one who made Trent sore, over at Wheelers', so I'm as much to blame as you are. Now turn off the waterworks before I disown you!" He turned briskly to Brian. "Am I right?"

"Check!" Brian said, nodding. Trixie dashed away the single tear and smiled gratefully at them both.

"This may all blow over if you children are careful about what you say the next few days," their father counseled soberly. "So let's keep our fingers crossed and hope that there'll be no more double-meaning stories in the *Sun.*"

"Yes, Dad," Trixie said, very subdued and worried.

More Trouble • 17

TRIXIE BOUNCED out of bed the moment she heard the delivery boy whistle at the gate. It was just getting light, and she had trouble locating one of her slippers, but within a few minutes, she was hurrying quietly downstairs and out the front door to get the paper.

She could hardly wait to get back to the house to look for a story under Paul Trent's by-line, but she made herself wait and ran back inside before she opened the *Sun*.

There was no story by him on the front page nor on any of the other pages. He was, she thought, with a load lifting off her heart, most happily absent. She was so relieved that she paid no attention to any other stories in the newspaper but folded it up neatly and left it at her father's place at the dining room table. Then she dashed upstairs to snatch a few minutes' more sleep before it was time to wake Bobby and get him dressed.

She was in high spirits as they all gathered around

the breakfast table a little later. In a few days, she hoped, if there were no more stories about Miss Rachel in the *Sun,* Sleepyside would forget about the whole thing, just as Dad had said.

"There's a council meeting scheduled for today," her dad was saying as he skimmed the second page of the paper. "Special session, this says, to discuss draining Martin's Marsh and starting to put that access road into work. I thought that had been postponed."

"I suppose the thing about Miss Rachel and Gaye was what reminded them of it," Mrs. Belden sighed.

"I'm afraid there's no question about that," her husband agreed with a frown.

"Will Miss Rachel have to sell her cottage and move away? Can the city make her?" Trixie was shocked.

"Actually, Miss Martin doesn't own any of that property any longer. The bank does."

"But how can that be? It's always belonged to her family!" Trixie argued indignantly.

"Unfortunately, Miss Rachel had to sign over all her rights to the property several years ago, after the changes in the roads had put an end to her rug and quilt business. For a while, she borrowed from the bank, but she found that she had no way to pay back her loan, so she insisted on signing over everything to the bank. The board planned to let her stay there as long as she lived, but now—" He shook his head gravely. "I only hope that this is just a flurry of talk in the council."

"But where will she move to if the council *does* start building that road?" Trixie asked unhappily. She still couldn't help feeling that she would be to blame if that happened. "They know she has no money to buy another place—probably not even enough to rent one."

"There are places where she can go if she wishes to," her father said, and he busied himself with breakfast.

Trixie turned to her mother for help. Moms looked uneasy and rose hastily to go and putter with something on the stove. "But where?" Trixie asked.

"I guess Dad means the Home," Brian said quietly.

"It's really quite a comfortable place," Mr. Belden said hastily, "and she would find people near her own age to keep her company. Excellent doctors, too, if she needed them."

Moms came back to the table, wearing the same stricken look that Trixie had. "But, Peter! A *Martin* in the Home!" she protested.

Mr. Belden looked uncomfortable. "Oh, Mother!" he said with gentle reproof. "It isn't like going to jail, dear. And you must realize how much better off Miss Rachel would be. At her age, out there far away from everyone as she is, almost anything could happen to her. A fall or a stroke! She could be sick for days before anyone found out about it."

"I suppose you're right," Mrs. Belden sighed.

"Well, she looks good and healthy to me." Trixie frowned rebelliously. "And I hope the council decides to forget all about that icky old access road for a long time!"

"To be truthful, so do I," her father admitted.

The Bob-Whites discussed it every time they had a chance to get together during the day, but none of them could think of any way to help Miss Rachel if the council decided to get started with the road.

It was Brian who heard the news first, from the councilman's son. The city council had voted unanimously to begin work on the access road not later than early fall. Jim and Brian told the girls and Mart the news as they hurried for the bus after school.

Trixie brightened, and her voice was almost a squeak as she asked, "Early fall? Oh, that'll give us all summer to find a way to help Miss Rachel so she won't have to go to the Home to live!"

"Maybe we could hold a square dance on the Fourth of July as a benefit for her!" Honey suggested eagerly.

"That's a gorgeous idea!" Trixie agreed.

But Brian and Mart and Jim all looked glum. "Oh, great!" Mart said witheringly. "That would make a hit with the city fathers, wouldn't it? A benefit to keep someone from having to go to the Home to live. After they've put a couple hundred thousand dollars of tax money into the new building there!"

"Forgetting that angle," Jim said seriously, "I'm pretty sure Miss Rachel would never hold still for a public benefit. From what I've heard of her, she has too much pride. I imagine she'd prefer to go quietly to the Home."

"I guess you're right, Jim," Trixie sighed, "but then, you most always are. We didn't stop to think."

Honey smiled at her. "Well, we have lots of time to think in all directions now," she told Trixie.

"Maybe longer than you expect," Brian said lightly. "All sorts of things could delay the start of work on the road. You know, red tape and stuff."

"Hooray for red tape!" Trixie exclaimed.

The rest of that day she was her usual happy self

and only thought of Miss Rachel a couple of times. One of them was when she and Honey were grooming Strawberry and Lady after a canter through the Wheeler woods and all around the lake. She was busy with the currycomb, and Honey was saddle-soaping Lady's gear. "Listen!" Trixie said, cocking her head in the direction of the house. "That poor child is still at it!"

Honey stopped work to listen to the distant strains of Gaye's violin. Over and over, the unseen violinist played the same passage of brilliant notes. "I wish I had a good big cup of hot mint tea from Miss Rachel's right now. I'd march right up to the music room and make that governess let poor Gaye rest and sip that tea. I know it would do her a lot of good."

Trixie nodded and grinned. "I wouldn't mind a dash of it right now, myself." Then she frowned thoughtfully. "I wonder what Miss Rachel's going to do about her herb garden when she has to give up the cottage. Just leave it there, I suppose, and let the city cover it with concrete."

"It's the rose garden I think she'll miss the most," Honey said. "Did you hear her telling Di that one of the first things she remembers is her great-grandmother Molly walking with her in that rose garden? She said her great-grandmother had a thick Irish brogue and always wore a white lace cap. She told her fabulous stories about Irish fairies and leprechauns and pookas, whatever they are."

"Leprechauns are fairy shoemakers only a few inches high," Trixie chuckled. "Pookas I've never heard of, but I bet Regan could tell us all about them. Dan, too."

"Which reminds me that we'd better get *these* pookas under blankets, or Regan will slay us both!" Honey said, and they hurried through the rest of the grooming with speed and concentration.

"A leprechaun would be fun to see," Trixie said when they had finished, "but I think I'd prefer to see a dragon, especially one with bright green beads for eyes and five claws on each foot."

"Goodness!" Honey teased. "I think I'll get in touch with Paul Trent and tell him there are rumors that Miss Trixie Belden has fallen in love with a gentleman dragon. He'd be sure to print it right on the front page!"

"And I wouldn't deny it!" Trixie laughed as they put the horses into their stalls and closed the barn doors. Then they said good night, and Trixie dashed home to her neglected duties.

The story of the council's decision to start the access road in the fall was headlined in the morning paper. Trixie, Mart, and Brian bent their heads over the paper to read it. "You were right, Brian," Trixie said happily. "It says they'll start *sometime* this fall. That's lots more vague than early fall. Maybe the next story will say *next spring!*"

"When will you learn that our ancient brother is always right?" Mart drawled, and then he ducked as Brian pretended to aim a fist at him.

The playful scuffle that followed was broken up by a sudden gasp from Trixie. "Hey, look at this! A story by Trent on page two about the Martins!"

Mart leaned over to read it with her, and Brian said,

"Come on, let's hear it! What's his mean little slant?"

Mart read aloud, " 'Recluse to leave historic property.' "

"He didn't waste much time spreading the news,"
Brian said grimly. "Go on."

"Miss Rachel Martin, he says, has been notified that
she has to move off the last piece of the once widespread
Martin holdings." Mart condensed it as he read. "He
mentions the fire and weeps a few crocodile tears over
the big house having been burned down forty years ago."

"Just gloating over poor Miss Rachel, I suppose, because she ran him away from her place for saying mean
things about her ancestors!" Trixie said, anger reddening
her cheeks.

"He has certainly dug into the family history. Probably got it out of the old *Sun-Courier* files at the newspaper morgue," Mart told them. "It seems that her
great-granddad was a miserly old coot who owned a
couple of trading ships that brought stuff from China."

"She has a gorgeous brass box her great-grandfather
imported from there," Trixie interrupted. "It has dragons
battling all over it—perfectly ferocious dragons. One has
green shiny eyes and five claws on each foot!"

"Sounds ugh to me!" Brian teased. "Go on with the
Martin family dirt, sonny boy."

"Well, it seems old Ezarach Martin had an only son,
by the same name, who fell in love with one of the maids,
named Melanie, and they ran off and got married. Old
Ez disowned him for it."

"What happened to him?" Trixie asked.

"Young Ez had one son and then was lost at sea,
when one of his father's schooners went down. He was

just a common seaman, working for wages, and the scandal around town was that he wouldn't have had even that job if his mother, Molly, hadn't made the old man give it to him. Trent's article says that Molly and the old man blamed each other because the boy was lost, but old Ez never softened enough to take young Ez's boy and his mother, Melanie, in to live with him and Molly. He started living like a miser and making Molly live that way, too."

"Poor Molly! She must have been brokenhearted," Trixie sighed.

"Maybe," Brian said. "All it says here is that after old Ez was gone, the little grandson and his mother came home to live. But nobody ever found any trace of the fortune Ez was supposed to have made from trading. If there was any, he certainly didn't leave any clues to its whereabouts."

"I wonder how much of this is fact and how much is Trent's fiction," Brian said musingly.

"Seems to me Miss Rachel could sue him if he made it up, especially calling her great-grandpa a miser," Trixie said indignantly. "I certainly would."

Brian looked over Mart's shoulder at the article. "I doubt if she could do anything about it. Trent covers himself very nicely by saying, 'It was rumored at the time' and 'The general opinion was.'"

"Pretty slick," Mart said with a disappointed sigh.

"I wonder if Melanie or her little boy, Miss Rachel's dad, ever found *any* of the fortune," Trixie said, knitting her brows.

"Trent says not. In fact, he seems to think it's still

there in the ruins. Hear ye!" Mart told her. " 'It would
be a strange ending to the Martin mystery if the wreck-
ing crews who pull down the ruins of those old mansion
walls were showered with a fortune in gold and silver
from some still-undiscovered hiding place!' " Mart tossed
the paper on the table with a chuckle. "Some imagination! As if that fire wouldn't have burned up any secret
doors or cabinets and left the gold and silver in the open!"

"I suppose it would have," Trixie conceded sadly.
Then she brightened again. "Maybe it was buried in the
cellar! It could still be there, under all the bricks and
dirt. And if we could dig down deep—"

"Hold it!" Mart threw up both hands. "You're not
about to hornswoggle us into going out there on Trent's
hunch and getting blisters for nothing!"

"Mart's right, Trix," Brian said hastily. "Remember
that both Melanie and her son, Rachel's father, must
have searched the house many times during the years
they lived there. And the first place they would have
looked would probably have been the cellar."

"I suppose so," Trixie conceded with a sigh. "Just
the same, I wish somebody could find it. It would be
wonderful to be able to hand it to Miss Rachel so she
could buy herself another little house, close to town,
and open up a handicraft shop or something."

"That's a nice little dream, Trix," Brian said, "but
I'm afraid you'll have to think up a more possible answer
for her. Miss Martin is in real trouble, and she needs
more than a dream to get her out of it."

Time Limit • 18

THE REST of the school week passed without any of the Bob-Whites being able to think of any way to help Miss Rachel avoid going to the Home to live.

"At least we have lots of time to rack our massive brains and come up with something spectacular," Trixie told Honey as they saddled up Lady and Strawberry for their Friday afternoon ride.

Honey nodded agreement. Then she said, "Do you think it would be all right for us to ride out that way this afternoon? I just had a horrible thought."

"What was that?" Trixie asked in a startled tone. She wasn't sure whether Honey was joking or not. But when she looked over Lady's back and saw her friend's face, she knew that Honey was serious.

"Why, here we've been fussing about Miss Rachel's having to go to the Home this fall, and nobody has even asked her how she's going to feel about it! Maybe she won't mind at all."

Trixie stared at her friend, her own eyes widening into two blue pools. "Honey! I never even gave that a thought! I guess we'd better find out before we get all steamed up about trying to keep her out of it!"

A few minutes later they were riding along Glen Road, in the direction of Miss Rachel's home.

They had gone only a short distance along the turnoff road, when they heard a sound like a car engine backfiring. It seemed to have come from up ahead on the old road.

"Somebody's old car is having a tough time getting up the road," Honey called over gaily to Trixie.

But Trixie, looking down from her saddle at the nearly dry road, suddenly drew in and stopped. "There are no tire tracks," she said. And just as she finished speaking, there was another distant sharp sound.

Honey, who had stopped when Trixie did, turned puzzled eyes to Trixie. "It sounded more like a shotgun. Dad took me duck hunting last fall, and his gun sounded just like that."

"But this is the closed season, and, anyway, this is within the city limits." Trixie frowned.

"It could be a poacher or some careless kid trying to be smart," Honey said worriedly. "Maybe we'd better just turn back. He could hit one of us or the horses by mistake."

"Oh, phoo!" Trixie growled. "I *hate* to turn back after we've come this far. My mouth was all set for mint tea."

"Mine, too," Honey sighed, "but there's no use taking chances on being mistaken for a deer by some goofy amateur hunter!"

They were turning their horses, when they heard voices of men coming from farther along up the road. The voices were loud and sounded angry.

"Let's duck," Trixie said quickly. "We can get behind those bushes and watch without being seen. Those fellows up ahead seem to be angry about something."

Honey didn't wait to discuss it. She wheeled Strawberry and headed the roan mare toward the bushes. Trixie was close behind her.

Now the men were coming around a bend in the narrow road. There were six of them, and they were rough-looking young fellows in denims, carrying long-handled spades and shovels over their shoulders. One of the men was limping and being supported by one of the others. They were all talking angrily about something, but neither of the girls could make out what it was that had upset them.

Trixie and Honey sat watching them disappear around the next curve. "They look as if they'd been digging," Trixie said in a carefully lowered voice.

"Maybe they've been digging in the swamp for that legendary pirate loot," Honey guessed.

But Trixie shook her head and said, "Nobody's been silly enough to do that in the past hundred years. Besides, their boots weren't muddy. I looked specially."

"Then, I wonder if—" Honey began but stopped abruptly. "That silly newspaper story about a fortune being hidden in the ruins of the Martin place! That must be what brought them here!"

"*Mr.* Trent again! I bet you're absolutely right!" Trixie exclaimed disgustedly.

"But I wonder what the shots were," Honey said, with a little shiver.

"There's only one way to find out," Trixie said soberly. "I think we should keep on. I have a funny sort of hunch about it. When we were at Miss Rachel's the other day, I noticed a double-barreled shotgun in a rack near the fireplace."

"Oh!" Honey exclaimed, horrified. "You surely don't think Miss Rachel would shoot at anyone, do you?"

"She might shoot over their heads to scare them away," Trixie answered. "I think we should find out right now what happened. She might be glad to see us."

"All right," Honey agreed, but weakly.

A moment later they were again on their way.

They stopped as they came to the ruined mansion. Footprints made by boots such as the men were wearing were all around the place. And when Trixie, on an impulse, dismounted and ran back to look at the rose garden, she found it a complete wreck. Bushes were broken, some were uprooted, signs of digging were at the foot of the mounds of rubble at the edge of the garden, and there was strong evidence that the men had been looking for something there.

She rejoined Honey and swung into her saddle. "They made a mess of the rose garden," she said, "but I didn't see a print of her little shoes anywhere around, so I guess they must have gone to her cottage, too. Let's hurry."

And they were on their way again, riding faster now.

Miss Rachel was standing in front of her open door, watching, as they rode in. She held the ancient shotgun at her side, but when she saw who they were, she set it against the doorway and went to meet them.

The girls dismounted quickly and hurried to the gate as Miss Rachel came down the path.

"Were those rough-looking men here, Miss Rachel?" Trixie called out as they came. A moment later she stared, speechless, at the condition of the garden. All the dainty spring flowers, in their neat little beds, had been trampled into the earth. Over in the side garden, the herbs were a mess of broken plants and boot marks. There was nothing left of the well-tended garden.

"They came for a drink at the well," Miss Rachel told the girls, her thin little face drawn and tragic, "and when I asked them to be careful of my wildlings and the spring beauties, they said it didn't matter about a bunch of weeds. And one of them even suggested that as long as they hadn't found any of my great-grandfather's gold in the ruins of the big house, they really should look inside my cottage. I told them to go, but they called me an old witch and a lot of other names. So I scared them away with my father's shotgun."

"How awful for you!" Honey exclaimed indignantly.

"One of the men was limping," Trixie said.

"I know." Miss Rachel almost managed a smile. "He was the one who was leading them, but when I brought out the shotgun, he was so frightened that he didn't wait to go out through the gate but jumped over it, and he sprained his ankle or his knee or something. The others argued about coming back, but I shot into the air a couple of times, and that ended the argument. I suppose they'll come back again, or others like them, now that there's been a rumor about hidden gold."

Though the girls did their best to convince her that Sergeant Rooney or some other police officer would take a hand in stopping the intrusion, Miss Rachel was still shaky as she remembered her manners and invited them in for mint tea.

It was over the cup of tea that Trixie finally got up courage to ask, "How soon do you have to move away, Miss Rachel?"

Miss Rachel's face looked haunted as she hesitated.

"Not for a long time, we hope," Honey put in quickly.

Miss Rachel flashed her a quick smile of gratitude. "I really don't know, exactly. Late in summer, I suppose. I hope that I can stay here until my pennyroyal and the bergamot are ready to gather—what those men have left alive, I mean."

"Pennyroyal. Isn't that a kind of mint? I think Miss Bennett mentioned it. For fever, isn't it?" Trixie said.

"Oh, yes! There's nothing quite so good for reducing a fever," Miss Rachel told them. "I have some left in my herb cabinet, but I like to gather it fresh every fall."

"I hope you can stay all fall and winter and just as long as you want to, Miss Rachel," Trixie said earnestly.

"Why, thank you both," Miss Rachel told them gratefully, but she sighed afterward. "Of course, the bank people seem to feel that the sooner I am away from here and settled in—" she paused a long moment, then went on bravely—"in some other place, the better it will be."

Both girls knew without asking that she meant the city's Home, and for a minute there was silence, except for the ticking of the old grandfather clock in the corner. It boomed out the hour of four and made Honey start with such surprise that it brought a giggle from Trixie.

"He's a noisy old fellow," Miss Rachel said lightly, "but he's company, even if he did get scorched in the fire."

Trixie went over to look more closely at the painted face of the old clock. "Goodness—1714! He *is* an old one," she exclaimed. She noticed the small drawer at the foot of the clock. "What's in there?"

"I'm sure I don't know. I never thought to open it," Miss Rachel said. "You may look, if you wish."

Trixie squatted down and pulled gently on the small porcelain knob. It resisted her effort to open the drawer.

"Hey, it's locked! Here's a keyhole, a little round one. What kind of a key would open that?"

Miss Rachel and Honey both went over to look, and Miss Rachel said quickly, "My father's gold watch was wound with a key of the same kind. I'll get it and see if it will fit this lock. I'm getting curious myself now." She hurried to her bedroom to look for the key.

"Wouldn't it be wonderful if she found that little drawer all filled with gold pieces! Wouldn't that be something to throw at Paul Trent!" Trixie chortled.

But when Miss Rachel had located the small key with its straight shaft and had tried it, there were three disappointed faces as the key turned loosely in the lock.

"I guess that's that," Trixie sighed. "I don't suppose you have a thicker key of the same kind."

"I'm afraid not," Miss Rachel said regretfully.

Trixie's blue eyes sparkled suddenly, and she reached over and pulled a bobby pin from one of Honey's long golden-brown tresses. "Let's turn burglar! I saw a girl in a TV show use one of these to open a door. Cross your fingers, everybody!"

And as both the elderly spinster and Honey solemnly watched, Trixie inserted the bobby pin in the small lock and wiggled it a couple of times. There was a tiny click as the drawer sprang open.

Three pairs of eyes stared into an empty space. There was silence for a long moment; then Trixie said glumly, "Empty!" Honey only groaned.

"Don't be disappointed, my dears. It would have been wonderful if we had found the drawer full of gold pieces, but it was asking too much. Those things only happen in fairy tales," Miss Rachel told them, with an attempt at a laugh. But the laugh sounded anything but real to Trixie and Honey, and they exchanged unhappy glances.

Almost at once, Trixie brightened. She faced Miss Rachel impulsively and asked, "Miss Rachel, when you leave here—I mean, when you go wherever you're planning to go—will you have room for all this furniture?"

"Why, I—I hadn't thought about it. I don't suppose I will have too much room there—I mean, where I'm going. Would you like the clock? I'd be happy to give it to you if you can use it," Miss Rachel said with a smile. "I'd like the old fellow to have a good home."

"Oh, no, I wasn't thinking of your *giving* it to me—or anybody," Trixie said eagerly. "I was thinking that, if you won't have room for these pieces, you could probably get a lot of money for them."

"Sell them?" Miss Rachel stared at her in surprise. "Why, I hadn't thought of that. I suppose I could."

"My mother paid two hundred dollars for a rosewood

desk not half as pretty as this one you have," Honey said quickly. "I know if you wanted to sell any of these lovely things, lots of people would be interested."

"Oh!" Trixie's blue eyes were round with excitement. "You could have an auction sale this fall, just before you have to move away! We Bob-Whites could help you by putting up posters and getting publicity for the sale, and Jim could be the auctioneer, because he's been studying about old Colonial furniture like yours and can tell how much to take for it, and—" But she had run out of breath and had to pause to catch a new supply before she could go on.

"We'll have lots of time to get ready for it." Honey took it up. "All summer! And I know the boys will be delighted to do all they can to help!"

"That's for sure!" Trixie nodded vigorously. "What do you say, Miss Rachel?"

"I'm speechless, girls," Miss Rachel said in a quavering voice, and she dabbed at her eyes with the daintiest of lace handkerchiefs. "I don't know how to thank you for being so kind." She hesitated a moment and then said, with sweet dignity, "It could make quite a difference if I had a few hundred dollars. I could rent a little place in town where I could display my quilts and rugs, and—" She was too choked up to continue.

Both girls knew what she had left unsaid—that the thought of independence would make all the difference.

"Well, you can depend on the B.W.G.'s to put it over. We'll get the boys busy on ideas right away," Trixie said, briskly businesslike to cover her sympathy. "And we'll keep in touch with you and let you know what we've worked out. It's going to be great fun for us." She looked quickly at her watch. "Oops! We're late, Miss Rachel. We have to go now." She pulled Honey by the arm. "Come on, or we'll be scalped by Regan for keeping the horses out so long!"

A moment later, they were running gaily down the path to their horses. When they mounted and turned the patient animals homeward, they looked back to wave at Miss Rachel as she stood looking after them.

She waved in return and then stood for a long time looking in the direction in which they were riding.

The two girls were surprised to see Jim and Brian talking seriously in front of the little clubhouse.

"They're probably plotting not to help us with the horses tonight!" Trixie giggled. "Wait till they hear the plans we've made! They'll be so thrilled that they'll insist on grooming these two themselves, out of sheer gratitude!"

But she was in for a shock. She and Honey hurried to the boys, fairly bubbling over with the report of their visit with Miss Rachel. But before they had finished telling their story, Jim stopped them.

"Sorry, kids," he said, "but Miss Rachel won't be around any longer at the end of summer. She has to move out of the cottage by a week from Sunday."

The Best-Laid Plans · 19

BUT WHY? Why does Miss Rachel have to move out of her cottage so soon?" Trixie asked, bewildered.

"Because the work on the road is to start in a couple of weeks, and they're closing off the road to the cottage a week from Monday," Brian explained.

"Oh, no!" Trixie and Honey said it at the same time and in the same shocked tone.

"Oh, yes," Jim contradicted grimly. "Brian's friend Bud—you know, the one whose father's on the council —Bud told Brian a few minutes ago that the council has changed its collective mind about waiting till fall to start cutting that road through the marsh. And apparently Miss Rachel herself is to blame!"

"I don't understand." Trixie frowned.

"It seems that your friend Miss Rachel Martin took a couple of shots at some young fellows who had stopped by her place and asked for a drink of water," Brian explained. "It happened this afternoon. Lucky you missed it. Must have been before you got there."

"It wasn't like that at all! They didn't ask for a drink. They dug up her rose garden first and then came and trampled all her lovely flower garden and called her an old witch!" Trixie said hotly. "Didn't they, Honey?"

Honey nodded solemnly. "We came along right after it happened, and she was still trembly. And she shot over their heads with an old, old shotgun, to scare them away when they wanted to come into her house and look for her great-grandfather's 'hidden gold' that Trent mentioned in the *Sun!*"

"That wasn't *their* story, and the council believed them. Now they're sure she's a menace to the neighborhood," Brian explained. "That's why they're making her move out before anything else can happen."

"Why can't we go to the police and make them listen to what really happened?" Trixie asked angrily.

"Too late. The council has already announced its decision. It's official. The deadline for her to get moved away would be a week from this Sunday," Brian said. "So if you can get ready for the sale, it'll have to be held on Saturday. And that's pretty short notice."

"That's right, Trix." Jim nodded. "Don't forget, there'll be posters to make and distribute and signs to letter so we can post the road that people will have to take to the marsh. Most of them don't know the way."

"And there's a little question of how we're going to advertise the sale, without spending money that we don't have in our treasury!" Brian warned.

"I know one way," Honey said eagerly. "I can get Mom and Dad to talk it up among their friends. Lots of the ladies from the Arts Club collect antiques like mad, and they're always trying to get ahead of each other at it."

"Good thinking, squaw," Mart said with a grin. They hadn't noticed that he had strolled up. "The Beldens might do their part, too. I'll put pressure on Moms for a new handmade quilt for my bed. The old one's getting worn out."

They all laughed but Trixie. She sniffed at her almost-twin. "If you didn't eat pizza in bed so much, it wouldn't have to be cleaned so often that it's getting worn out!"

"That settles you, young feller!" Brian told him. "But let's decide, right now, whether we hold the sale or the girls have to tell Miss Rachel it's too much for the Bob-Whites to handle."

"What do you think, Jim?" Trixie asked of her co-president.

"I'm for it," Jim said seriously. "I think, with everybody working hard, we can pull it off. How about starting right in tonight? We'll have a meeting at the clubhouse as soon as we get through dinner and our evening chores, and we'll map it out like a battle campaign."

When the mapping was done and each of them knew exactly what he or she would have to get done by the day of the sale, it didn't look so forbidding. Trixie and Honey and Di were to ride out to Miss Rachel's as often as possible to help her pack. They were to spread the word at school about the sale, so their classmates could tell about it at home.

The boys were to letter the posters and tack them up on fences and trees, where it was allowed, and then get the direction markers ready for the morning of the sale.

"The main thing," Trixie warned the others, "is not to say anything about how badly Miss Rachel needs the money. It's just a closing-out sale. I think that's what they call it."

"Trix is right. No use letting everybody know that she's hard up. They'll want the stuff for practically nothing," Mart said promptly.

"I didn't think of that," Trixie admitted, frowning. "I was just thinking that it would hurt Miss Rachel if people knew." She sent Jim an appealing glance.

"Agreed! So no sob stuff, kids," Jim said crisply.

"Okay, okay," Mart growled, "but I hope Paul Trent doesn't make a big thing of it."

"I'm pretty sure he won't," Jim said grimly. "Dad knows the editor of the *Sun* pretty well, and after Trent wrote that stuff about the Martins, Dad filled the editor in on Trent's motives. Mr. Trent is now under orders to lay off Miss Martin, from any angle."

"Well, thank goodness for that!" Trixie sighed, and Honey seconded her.

"And now, let's get the ice carnival posters off the shelf and see how many we can salvage for the sale. It'll save us a lot of time—and money—if we can use them again," Brian suggested.

They were all soon at work on the posters and planning the next day's schedule. Dan Mangan wouldn't be able to do as much as the others, because his chores at Mr. Maypenny's kept him very busy from early morning till late at night, with only enough time off to attend school and study. He was very happy living at the old farm, as Mr. Maypenny was giving his young assistant more and more responsibility, now that Dan had learned to like the life and had put the past behind him. He had left the meeting early, but he had promised to drop over when he had a chance during the week and do what he could to get ready for the sale.

"I think Trix and I should take a run out to see Miss Rachel tomorrow and tell her what we are planning," Honey said as the meeting broke up.

"Good idea," Trixie agreed. "She probably needs some good news, after finding out that she has to move away so soon."

"I think I'll go along and take a look at that furniture you two have been raving about. I hope I can guess close to what it would be worth," Jim said.

"And I think I'll ride with you, too," Mart said, with a casual wave of his hand. "Might as well decide where to nail up these route arrows." He indicated the small wooden slats, shaped like arrows, that he had been lettering. "Get an idea how many more to make."

"I'll bring the lunch," Di said demurely, "if I'm free in the morning." She batted her eyelashes at Mart.

"Gosh, that's swell!" Mart beamed. "We'll stop by for you, then."

"Let's see, there'll be six of us and Miss Rachel." Brian counted on his fingers.

"Six? You going, too?" Mart asked with a frown.

"Why, of course, sonny boy! I may not know much about the price of antiques and where to put direction signposts, but I sure do love those chicken sandwiches Di's cook makes!" Brian chuckled teasingly.

But in the morning, as they saddled up at Honey's and got ready to ride by Di's, leading a mount for her, it looked as if the party might be increased by one.

Gaye was there, looking very thin and tired but also very determined. She had Mr. Poo draped over her arm, as usual, and she was demanding that Regan saddle Lady for her so she could go with the others.

"But, Miss Gaye"—Regan was being very gentle with her—"your aunt told me that you weren't to ride anymore because it tired you too much."

Gaye stamped her foot angrily. "I don't care! I want to go and see our friend Miss Rachel. She likes Mr. Poo and me to come to see her. She said so."

Trixie looked down at the angry little face and saw that Gaye was close to tears. Poor little thing! They had hardly had a glimpse of her all week. Impulsively, Trixie slid out of her saddle and went to her.

"We're only going to stay out there a little while," she explained. "There's something we have to arrange with Miss Rachel. This is a sort of business call."

Gaye looked sullen. Then she dashed away the tears with the back of her hand, and her thin little jaw set. "I know where you're going! You're going to go out there and dig up the gold that her great-grandpa hid. I know all about it!"

Trixie was surprised. "Oh, come now, Gaye! There isn't any such thing! Whoever said that is silly!"

"That's what you said about the pirate treasure. You always say that. And I don't believe you! Mitzi, my maid, says that cook told her—" She stopped abruptly as Mart laughed; she turned her glare on him. "And you needn't think you can fool me by laughing!" She turned and ran up the driveway and around the side of the garage.

They all sat for a moment, staring after her, and then, as Trixie climbed into her saddle again, Jim said seriously, "What was that all about? I mean the pirate treasure thing. I know where the maid got the rest of the yarn."

"Why, on our way back from Miss Rachel's the other day in the limousine, we happened to mention that old legend about the pirate loot that dopey people used to think was buried in the swamp. Gaye got all excited and said the oddest thing. Didn't she, Honey?" Trixie turned to her friend.

"That's right. She said she wouldn't be afraid to look for the pirate gold in the swamp and she was sure she and Mr. Poo could find it," Honey explained.

"That's just the usual kid talk," Brian chuckled. "What's so odd about that?"

"That wasn't what I meant," Trixie told them soberly. "It was what she said afterward. She said she'd dig up the gold and give it to her Aunt Della, and then she wouldn't ever have to play her old violin again or go traveling all the time when she was tired!"

"That was only kid stuff, too, Trix," Mart told her.

"No," Trixie said. "After she said it, she put her face down on the puppy's head, and I know she cried most of the way back to Honey's."

"Tired out, poor kid," Jim said, his green eyes darkening with sympathy. "That greedy aunt of hers. . . ."

They rode on then, a bit gloomy and silent. But the

gloom disappeared when they saw Miss Rachel's happy face as they told her their plans for the next Saturday's sale.

"You are all dear, dear children," she told them with a little catch in her voice, "and I know the sale will be very successful."

"My mother will be here," Di said as she spread out the lunch on Miss Rachel's kitchen table. "She adores antiques."

"Mine, too, I suspect." Honey laughed and added, "And most of the ladies of the Arts Club—all looking for bargains."

"Which they won't get." Jim grinned. "Now that I've seen what's here, I can just about guarantee that, instead of hundreds of dollars, you'll have a couple of thousand by the time the day's over."

"Oh, I hope so," Miss Rachel said breathlessly.

They all silently echoed her words.

When they dismounted at the Wheeler stable a little later, they found Gaye waiting for them. She ran to meet them, shouting, "Did you find the miser's gold? Where did he hide it? Let me see, right now!"

Trixie slipped out of her saddle. "We didn't go looking for *anybody's* gold, because we know there couldn't possibly be any! We didn't even go near the old ruins!"

"I don't believe you!" Gaye frowned.

"We did bring you something, though," Honey said with a smile, holding out a bouquet of sweet violets to Gaye. "Miss Rachel picked the very last of her flowers for you."

The scowl faded as Gaye put out her hand to take the violets. "Th-thank you, Honey," she said gravely. "They are very pretty." Then she turned away and went toward the house, carrying the flowers carefully in both hands.

"I really believe something touched that little heart of stone," Mart said, "at last."

Trixie sighed. "I wish she'd quit talking about that hidden gold. First thing you know, I'll believe it myself and probably break my fool neck climbing around that silly place looking for it!" She looked away thoughtfully.

Honey stared at her. She knew Trixie. "Don't you dare try it!" she said severely.

Trixie laughed. "I was talking to myself. Please excuse!"

"Well, tell yourself something else, dreamer—like Moms is probably fit to be tied right now. I heard her make a date at the beauty parlor for this afternoon at three, and if you don't get home to take Bobby off her hands, there's going to be one wrecked beauty parlor in Sleepyside!" Mart pointed an accusing finger at her.

"Gleeps! Thanks for reminding me!" And she dashed into the stable, dragging patient Strawberry after her.

Complications · 20

GETTING READY for the sale turned out to be a lot more work than any of the Bob-Whites had thought it would be. There were the old trunks to go through, discarded things to dispose of for Miss Rachel, and a great deal of packing. In addition, the furniture that was to be sold had to be polished and gotten into the best condition possible. And the posters had to be finished.

They had only two or three evenings free to go out there and lend a hand as a group, but Trixie managed to wheedle Brian into taking her almost every evening. Sometimes they picked up Di to go along; sometimes it was Honey who was free. And they all worked hard.

Finally it was Friday night, and everything seemed ready for the big day to come. They were exhausted. Trixie sat down by the rosewood desk and looked at the dragon box with loving eyes. "Somebody will buy you, my lovely monster," she said, patting the top dragon fondly. "I hope he likes you as much as I do."

"Loopy! That's what my sister is," Mart's voice came from the kitchen doorway. "Talks to dragons. Can't tell me she isn't a witch!"

Trixie made a face at him, lifted the heavy box down to the flat surface of the desk, and started to lower the desk lid. The lid slipped from her fingers and banged down hard on the base. Then she caught her breath. "Mart, come quick! Look!"

With a slight scraping noise, a small door swung out from the carved side of the desk. Until that moment, the carving had shown no crack, but now a whole section of the pattern came open. "It's a secret door!" Trixie exclaimed.

"Concealing diamonds and pearls, I hope!" Di exclaimed as she and the others hurried in to see what had made Trixie call out.

But when the door was opened to its full width, the only thing visible inside the compartment was a thin packet of letters in yellowed envelopes with strange, foreign stamps on them. Silk cord tied the packet, and an ancient twig of some sort of scented wood was caught in it.

They gathered around hopefully as Miss Rachel, as excited as anyone, took out the letters and glanced at them. "A Chinese stamp," she said, puzzled, and undid the knot in the silk cord.

They all held their breath as she scanned the single page of the first letter. "Why, it's only a letter from my great-grandfather Ezarach to his bride, Molly. He says he's sending her a gift of great price on their first wedding anniversary—" She read for a moment in silence, with a tender smile, and then again became conscious of the ring of young faces. "He says he has seen many strange things but never anything like this, and he hopes it will guard her safely till his return." She read a little more in silence, then, "And he closes, hoping that the scent of the sandalwood will remind her of the incense of their wedding day." She sighed.

"Probably a bottle of myrrh, whatever that is," Di said dreamily. "Why don't people write romantic things like that nowadays?"

"Wonder what he meant by guarding her," Trixie said. "Hey!" She brightened. "I bet it was a pistol all inlaid with pearl, or a sword with a golden hilt. Wonder what became of it!"

"I'm afraid that's something we will never know now," Miss Rachel said with a little sigh. "This letter must be close to a hundred years old."

"Gleeps!" Trixie said and then lapsed into gloom.

"We'd better leave pretty soon," Brian reminded them. "Tomorrow's going to start awfully early and last a long time."

"Before you go," Miss Rachel told them, "I want you to know that no matter how the sale turns out tomorrow, I'll never forget the kindness of all of you."

"That's okay," Brian said hastily, his dark cheeks blushing with embarrassment. "Come on, squaws. You going to hang around all night?"

Brian hustled them out to the car without ceremony, but when they were safely in, Mart still hadn't come out of the cottage. "Mart!" he yelled and honked.

A moment later, Mart came scurrying out, carrying a

newspaper-wrapped bundle under his arm.

"What's that?" Brian asked crossly.

"Could be a bread box, but it isn't," Mart answered saucily, making the girls giggle. "And I don't want any of you trying to peek at it. Get me?"

"Oh, who wants to?" Trixie retorted, but under her flippancy she was excited. She felt sure she could guess what was in that package, and she meant to find out as soon as Mart had hidden it. She knew most of his hiding spots, though he had never suspected it.

Miss Martin had asked her several times to pick out a gift for herself among the antique furnishings of the cottage, but Trixie had insisted that she didn't want a thing. Only Honey could have guessed what Trixie really wanted, or maybe Mart himself, after their little exchange tonight.

She felt sure it was to be a birthday gift. Her four-teenth birthday was only a week away now, but she couldn't wait. She had to see her box again tonight.

"What do you suppose is in that package?" Honey asked in a whisper.

"Goodness!" Trixie pretended to cover a yawn. "How can I guess what silly secret my little twin might have?"

She said it loudly enough for Mart to hear, but all she got from him in answer was a dry "Don't you wish you could?" which made Honey and Di both giggle and also made Trixie sure she had guessed right.

"Why don't you try three guesses?" Mart jibed.

But Trixie was too happy to bother to answer. At the moment she was trying to decide just where she would keep the dragon box in her room. Somewhere up high, out of Bobby's reach till he grew older, of course.

Brian stopped the car on the sloping driveway and left it pointed down toward the road, so they could roll down to start the motor instead of making a racket with the ancient starter. They would be leaving early.

Mart got out and took the mysterious package into the house with him. Trixie followed him in, wishing she could say, "Let me carry my dragon box." But that would spoil the surprise, so she didn't say it.

Their parents were still up and waiting to hear how things were going out at the Martin cottage.

Mart put down his package and poured himself a glass of milk at the refrigerator. "Everything's great, except Jim can't be there," he said. "But he's given Trix and Honey and Miss Rachel herself a list of prices to ask, so they don't really need an auctioneer. Of course, I could have done it, but—"

"I'm glad you decided not to," his father said dryly. "The fact is, I'll need both you and Brian here all day. We've got to get the kitchen garden planted for Moms; the weather report says we'll have rain by Sunday."

"Suits me." Mart grinned. "Saves a lot of hard labor moving the furniture out to the shopping ladies' station wagons. Let 'em bring their own muscle guys!"

"Check!" Brian agreed. "I'll drop the girls out there and come back."

None of them noticed Bobby, in his sleepers, come to the kitchen door, sleepily rubbing his eyes. He stood yawning a moment, then spotted Mart's package and made a beeline for it. He climbed up on a chair and started tearing off the newspaper wrapping.

Trixie heard the paper rattle. "Bobby!" she exclaimed and made a dash for him. "Leave my dragon box alone!"

Bobby was so startled that he gave a hard pull on the newspaper, and the box slid off onto the floor.

"My box! My box!" Trixie wailed and fell to her knees to gather it up. "If you've broken it—"

"What's going on?" Mr. Belden asked sharply. Mart was standing with a baffled expression on his face, and Brian was frowning puzzledly.

"I guess I should have known that nobody can keep a secret around here," Mart growled. "Okay, take your silly brass box. It's a birthday present from Miss Rachel. But, for the love of pete, don't let her know you've got it now, way ahead of time. She'll be disgusted!"

"Don't worry. I won't!" She hugged the box to her. "It's going to go right on the highest shelf in my room, and I won't even think about it till my birthday!"

"I don't like the idea of your taking *any* presents from Miss Rachel," her father said, with a little frown, "but I suppose it would hurt her feelings if you took it back. And it's not anything that would bring her more than a couple of dollars at the sale. So. . . ." He shrugged.

"Dad, you're just the best!" Trixie beamed at him. "Good night, everybody! See you in the morning!" And she fled out into the hall and up to her room before anyone had a chance to have a second thought.

In the morning she was up at daybreak and lost no time shaking Brian awake. "Up!" she ordered. "I'll fix breakfast and call Honey and Di to get ready. Hurry!"

"Why," he groaned sleepily, "did I ever let myself be

talked into playing chauffeur for a bevy of females?"

"Because one of them has bee-yootiful hazel eyes! And it isn't me!" And she dashed out into the hall so fast that the pillow Brian hurled missed her.

By the time they were dressed and had snatched a quick bite of coffee cake and a glass of milk, full daylight had arrived. But it was a gray morning, and over in the east the clouds were dark and threatening.

"There's that storm that's due here tomorrow," Trixie said as they rode along Glen Road in the jalopy. "It looks kind of close, to me."

"I hope it holds off," Brian said, turning up into Honey's driveway. Then he stepped on the brake suddenly as two figures came down the drive from the house. "Hey, look! Gaye!"

"Carrying Mr. Poo like a stuffed doll, poor guy," Brian chuckled. "And what's that in her other hand? Looks like a suitcase."

Trixie jumped out of the car and ran to meet them. "Good morning, Gaye. Aren't you up early for a young lady who's playing a concert tonight?" she asked gaily.

Honey said quickly, "She's going with us."

"Oh-oh!" Trixie said doubtfully. "Does Miss Crandall know about it?"

"Of course she does!" Gaye scowled. "I told her I was going to the sale, and she said—" she seemed to be looking for the right word—"she told me, 'Go ahead, but be sure to be back early.'"

The two girls and Brian exchanged looks, but Gaye didn't wait. She climbed into the front seat next to Brian and settled down determinedly.

"And what's in there?" Brian asked, nodding toward the small suitcase.

"Oh, just Mr. Poo's lunch. He's on a very special diet— for his nerves, you know."

"First time I ever heard of that," Brian said, laughing softly. He beckoned to the two girls, who were still standing, undecided, beside the car. "Climb in and let's go."

They picked up Di at her gate, and she crowded in with Honey and Trix. Gaye was very silent in the front seat as Trixie told Di about Bobby and the brass box. She yawned a couple of times and then let her head fall against Brian's arm. When it stayed there in spite of the bumpy road, Brian realized that the tired little girl was sound asleep.

Even after they stopped at Miss Rachel's gate, she slept on. Brian gathered her up in his arms and took her inside the cottage, the small poodle close behind.

"Oh, the poor baby!" Miss Rachel whispered, seeing the drawn little face. "Put her down on the couch and let her have her sleep out."

Brian would have liked to stay awhile, but he knew he was needed at home, so after a few minutes and a handful of Miss Rachel's raisin cookies, he left.

A quarter of an hour later, a light rain was falling. Trixie stuck her nose out to look at the clouds and saw that they were much darker now and swirling across the sky. "Gleeps!" she thought. "I hope they keep right on going and it clears up, or nobody'll come to the sale."

But instead of slackening, the sprinkle became a downpour. Even Miss Rachel, who had been trying hard to pretend that she wasn't worried, looked glum. Gaye slept on, with Mr. Poo across her feet.

"Well, here we sit," Di said after a while. "Isn't there something we can still do?"

"I'm afraid we've done everything," Miss Rachel said with a sigh, "except getting together those packages of herbs I promised you girls for your botany class."

"Well, let's do that!" Honey said briskly. "Where do we find them?"

"Come along to the potting shed, and I'll put you all to work," Miss Rachel told them. "Here." She reached into the linen drawer of the sideboard. "Aprons for all!" When the girls had put them on and tied the wide, starched strings into bows for each other, they tiptoed out and left Gaye sleeping quietly, Mr. Poo at her feet.

In spite of the pouring rain outside, the girls had a good time for the next half hour, wrapping and labeling the Oswego tea leaves, the pennyroyal, and the other mints, like spearmint and horehound.

It was Trixie who thought she heard Mr. Poo barking. The others were busy with the herbs, so she threw her sweater over her head and started out. "I think I'll see how Gaye's getting along," she said hastily and dashed for the cottage. As she hurried along, she looked toward the front of the house, hopefully, for a car. But there was no car—only sheets of rain.

And when she was inside the cottage and hurried to check on little Gaye, there was no sign of the child. The dog was gone, too, and the small leather suitcase that Gaye had jealously guarded.

Trixie's Treasure • 21

TRIXIE RAN to the cottage door and flung it open. The small white gate was standing ajar. It was evident that Gaye had gone out that way. But which direction had she taken? Had she gone to the marsh or to the ruins?

"I've got to find her," Trixie told herself desperately. "That silly story about the miser's gold could be why she's gone—or it could be that old yarn about pirate loot in the swamp!" She felt sure now that Gaye hadn't been sound asleep on the couch. She must have waited till they were out of the room and then stolen out with her little suitcase. "It probably was empty. She was fibbing about Mr. Poo's lunch being in it! And now I'm sure she never even asked Miss Crandall if she could come with us. She must have sneaked away!"

Trixie hurried out to the gate. The rain was coming down so hard now that there was no chance of seeing any footprints pressed into the muddy road.

Then she heard the poodle barking. The sound was

coming from the direction of the ruins of the old Martin
mansion. Trixie started running as fast as she could
against the driving rain and gusty wind.

"I hope she hasn't had time to go far," she thought
uneasily, "but I guess not. I wouldn't have heard Mr.
Poo barking so clearly if they were very far away."

She hadn't gone a hundred feet more before she saw
the little dog running toward her, a soggy, small white
bundle that barked excitedly and then stopped, turned,
and seemed to be trying to urge her to follow him. "Okay,
Mr. Poo, I'm coming!" she called and went after him as
fast as she could. The poodle splashed his way ahead of
her, only stopping a couple of times to see if she was still
following.

He led her around past the old mansion and to the
rose garden. But there was no sign of Gaye. The mounds
of earth that the intruders had piled up in their digging
for treasure were now sodden masses of mud and stones,
and a stream of water was rushing past, down over the
stone steps that their digging had uncovered. The steps
led into what must have been the root cellar, near the
summer kitchen, where the fire had started. Trixie peered
down into the darkness. She could see that the lowest
step was awash.

"Gaye?" she called uncertainly and was relieved when
there was no answer. The little girl was probably climbing around in another part of the ruins.

Trixie started to turn away, but as she did, the small
dog came and stood at the edge of the steps and looked
down at the water, whimpering. "Oh, no!" Trixie whispered. "If she's down there, something must have hap-

pened to her." She called again. "Gaye! Are you down
there?" Again there was no reply.

Trixie hesitated only a second more and then began
to descend the steps. Mr. Poo started to follow her, but
Trixie ordered sternly, "Stay there!" and he lay down,
paying no attention to the rain that drenched his tiny
body but watching her and whining a little.

Gaye was in the cellar. But it was no fake faint this
time that kept her from answering Trixie. She had gone
down the steps, slipped, and fallen into the water, striking
her head. By some miracle, her face was still above water,
but most of her body was under. In a few minutes more,
she would have drowned.

Afterward, back at the cottage, Trixie could hardly
remember how she had been able to struggle against
the force of the rushing water, carrying Gaye's limp body
and inching along the rocky sides of the old cellar toward
the steps and safety. It was like a nightmare now, but
somehow she had done it and brought Gaye back to
consciousness in the shelter of a wildly swaying tree.

They had staggered hand in hand back to the cottage,
with the drenched puppy trotting ahead in the downpour. At the door, Miss Rachel had caught Gaye in her
arms as the child collapsed from excitement and fatigue.

Now, with Gaye safely tucked in bed but babbling
with a high fever, and Mr. Poo, rubbed dry and fluffy,
sleeping at her side, Trixie sat bundled in a blanket
before the fire. Honey hovered about her anxiously.

"Are you sure I can't get anything for you?" she asked.

Trixie shook her head quickly and sipped the spearmint

tea Miss Rachel had brewed for her. "Huh-uh. How's Gaye?"

"Miss Rachel says the Oswego tea should break her fever soon," Honey assured her. "She owes her life to you."

"Not me!" Trixie protested and meant it. "Mr. Poo did that. I had to save her, or he'd have bitten me!" And she changed the subject quickly. "I hear a car! Maybe it's a customer, at last! I'd better get out of sight!" She headed for the bedroom, trailing the blanket, as Di and Honey dashed for the door and excitedly peered out. But it wasn't a customer. It was Miss Della Crandall in Brian's jalopy. She came storming up the walk, her face dark with anger and determination.

"Where is my niece?" she demanded, pushing her way in.

"She's in the bedroom there," Honey told her quietly. "She's quite sick, Miss Crandall."

"Nonsense! I know her spiteful little tricks! She's pretending to be sick so she won't be punished for running away again!" Miss Crandall shoved the girls aside and stalked toward the bedroom door.

But before she could reach it, Trixie came out, still wrapped in the blanket, and shut the door quietly behind her. She stood resolutely in front of the closed door. "I heard what you said, Miss Crandall, and you're all wrong. Gaye didn't run away for spite. She hoped she could find some hidden gold she heard the servants gossiping about."

"Hidden gold? Ridiculous! Gaye earns a small fortune every year with her violin!" Miss Crandall said haughtily.

"Why would she want more?"

"To give you, so she wouldn't have to work so hard all the time," Trixie said very coldly and accusingly.

For a moment, Miss Crandall stared at Trixie. Then she covered her face with her hands and sank down into the nearest chair. They saw her shoulders shake and knew she was crying silently.

Honey and Di looked at each other helplessly, and Di said softly, "Oh, Trixie!"

But Trixie stood her ground, frowning. She told herself she wasn't sorry. It was time Miss Crandall heard the truth.

Gaye's aunt sat up straight suddenly, and, in spite of the tears that still wet her cheeks, she managed a smile. "I didn't know how she felt. I was being stern with her for her own sake. There's a reason—"

"You don't have to explain, Miss Crandall," Trixie interrupted hurriedly. "I'm sorry I was so outspoken."

"No, you were right to tell me. But I want you to know why I was so strict. You see, her father—my only brother—was a great violinist. But he was undisciplined all his life, and he died in poverty. I made up my mind Gaye would have something that couldn't be wasted when she grew up. Every cent she has made, except for our expenses, is in a trust fund for her. She'll never be penniless."

"Maybe if you told her . . ." Honey said softly. She was remembering how she and her mother had misunderstood each other before Trixie had come into their lives.

"Someday, when she's a little older, I will," Miss

Crandall said with a sigh. "Meanwhile, I've already canceled tonight's recital. And now"—she looked at Trixie thoughtfully—"after talking to you, I intend to call off the rest of our tour. I want Gaye to have a long vacation, while we both learn to be a real family and not just an artist and her manager." She smiled fleetingly. "You see, I really love my niece, though I haven't shown her so, I'm afraid."

The bedroom door opened then, and Miss Rachel came out, smiling. "The child is going to be all right," she told Miss Crandall. "The tea has broken her fever."

"I'd like to see my niece," Miss Crandall said humbly.

"She has been asking for you," Miss Rachel told her. "Please go in." And she stood aside as Miss Crandall hurried into the bedroom and closed the door.

"I think she may want to stay till Gaye can be moved," Miss Rachel told them. "So perhaps you children had better start for home before the rain gets any worse."

"But some customers might come—" Trixie began.

"Not a chance," Brian said from the front doorway. "We barely got through. I'm afraid the sale is a big flop, Miss Rachel."

Miss Rachel gave a deep sigh. "I suppose it's all for the best, after all. Even if a lot of people had come, they might have bought only a couple of the pieces. It would only have put off for a short time my going to the Home."

And since they had no argument to offer to that, the disappointed little group of Bob-Whites soon left for their homes, promising to come tomorrow after church to help her move her things to storage and herself to the Home, where a place would be waiting for her.

That night Trixie was wide-awake and restless half the night, trying to think of some way to help Miss Rachel escape what seemed to be her inevitable fate.

When she couldn't sleep by midnight, she took the brass box down from the shelf and stole downstairs with it. "Might as well be busy doing something, instead of fussing and worrying," she thought. The box's dullness had bothered her. She would shine it up.

She set to work on it and was startled to see the dull, brassy look disappear under the polish. A rich golden glow took its place. "It's almost like gold," she thought aloud. And then, as she tried to pry a small dark spot off the polished surface with the end of a nail file, her hand slipped, and the file made a deep scratch in the cover. The metal seemed very soft. It might really be gold!

Trixie felt sudden excitement. She rubbed harder with the polish. "What if it is real gold?" she wondered. And she thought at once, "Dad might know!"

In a flash she was out of the kitchen and running up the stairs to her parents' room. "Dad!" she called softly. "Please, there's something important!"

"Come in, Trixie!" Her father and mother were sitting by the window enjoying the moonlight that had followed the heavy rain. "What's bothering you at this hour?"

"My box! I'm almost sure it's gold, not brass! Won't you please come and see?"

"But it can't be gold, dear. Didn't Miss Rachel say it was brass?" her mother asked gently.

"She didn't say what it was. I don't think she'd know, because it belonged to her great-grandfather, and it came from China. Oh, Dad, please come and look at it!"

"We'll both come," he agreed. "I need a glass of milk, anyway, so the effort won't be wasted."

They followed Trixie as she dashed back downstairs to the kitchen. She pointed triumphantly to the box. "Look!"

"Goodness!" Mrs. Belden stared at the shining box in astonishment.

"It does look like gold, now that it's shined up," Trixie's dad conceded. "Tell you what. We'll take it to a jeweler some day next week and let him tell you."

"But, Dad, if it *is* gold, it would be wonderful to know before Miss Rachel has to move to the Home tomorrow. It could change everything!" she argued desperately.

"It could be just gold-plated, dear," her mother said sympathetically. "Don't build your hopes up too high, with so very little to go on."

"Wait, Moms! Dad! Remember the letter we found in the desk out there? It spoke about the 'thing' that was so strange-looking that he was sending her. It could be the fighting dragon! And he mentioned the scent of sandalwood. Moms, *you* know how sandalwood smells! Doesn't this have that smell?"

Mrs. Belden bent swiftly over the open box and then straightened with wide-eyed surprise. "Why, so it does, dear!"

"Then why can't this be the anniversary gift 'of great price' that he was sending her?" Trixie's blue eyes sparkled.

"Trixie, you really may have solved another puzzle! We'll drive in to see my friend Sam Lee Fong tomorrow morning and show that box to him. If anybody can tell us what it's worth, it will be Sam. He has an A-one standing with the Metropolitan Museum of Art as an expert on Chinese art," Mr. Belden said.

The next morning, Honey went with Trixie and her father to the city. Tom Delanoy drove them, and Trixie carried the box in her lap all the way.

But when they came back, except for a short stop to pick up Di, they went directly to Miss Rachel's, where the boys were hard at work loading furniture on a rented truck.

The Chinese expert's verdict was soon told to Miss Rachel, though Trixie found it hard to speak over the lump in her throat. *The Museum would pay several thousand dollars for such a perfect specimen of the art of the T'ang Dynasty of a thousand years ago.*

It was an afternoon of happiness for the Bob-Whites. To make it complete, the mayor and his four councilmen came out to call on Miss Rachel and explain a bit sheepishly that they had acted hastily in ordering the work on the road to commence so soon.

"You are welcome to stay till next summer now," the mayor told Miss Rachel. "We have found that we were misinformed as to conditions here."

"You're very kind," Miss Rachel told the gentlemen with great dignity, "but I would like to move into a small home in town, with a shop of my own, as soon as possible—to start my own business again. Thank you, just the same."

To cap the whole adventure, after school on Trixie's

birthday, there was a gay party for her in the clubhouse, complete with a gorgeous birthday cake. Miss Rachel was there, and there was a box with a beautiful orchid corsage and a card that said, "With love, Gaye and Aunt Della."

Best of all, the Bob-Whites were all there, and to make the day practically perfect, Mart pulled her curls and called her his "twin" in front of everyone, because now, for a whole month, they were both fourteen.

It was a happy but tired Trixie who tumbled into bed much later. So much had happened in the last few days that her head was whirling. But she wasn't too sleepy to wonder what adventure lay ahead—and whether her life at fourteen could possibly be as exciting as it had been during this wonderful year just ending.

β